Praise for *The Rare Coin Score* and Richard Stark

“The caper novel, the story of a major [illegible] operation from the point of view of the participants, has no better practitioner than Richard Stark. *The Rare Coin Score* . . . is an unusually good caper even for Stark’s hard-bitten professional thief, Parker. The million-dollar heist of an important numismatic convention is clean and sharp in its prose, plotting and characterization, and it is nicely twisted in its surprises.”

—Anthony Boucher, *New York Times Book Review*

“Richard Stark’s Parker . . . is refreshingly amoral, a thief who always gets away with the swag.”

—Stephen King, *Entertainment Weekly*

“Richard Stark’s Parker novels, a cluster of which were written in an extraordinary burst of creativity in the early ’60s, are among the most poised and polished fictions of their time and, in fact, of any time.”

—John Banville, *Bookforum*

“Gritty and chillingly noir . . . [Westlake] succeeds in demonstrating his total mastery of crime fiction.”

—*Booklist*

“The Parker novels . . . are among the greatest hard-boiled writing of all time.”

—*Financial Times* (London)

"If you're looking for crime novels with a lot of punch, try the very, very tough novels featuring Parker by Donald E. Westlake (writing as Richard Stark). [They] are all beautifully paced [and] tautly composed."

—James Kaufmann, *Christian Science Monitor*

"Westlake is among the smoothest, most engaging writers on the planet." —*San Diego Tribune*

"Elmore Leonard wouldn't write what he does if Stark hadn't been there before. And Quentin Tarantino wouldn't write what he does without Leonard. . . . Old master that he is, Stark does them all one better."

—*L.A. Times*

"Westlake's ability to construct an action story filled with unforeseen twists and quadruple-crosses is unparalleled."

—*San Francisco Chronicle*

"What chiefly distinguishes Westlake, under whatever name, is his passion for process and mechanics. . . . Parker appears to have eliminated everything from his program but machine logic, but this is merely protective coloration. He is a romantic vestige, a free-market anarchist whose independent status is becoming a thing of the past."

—Luc Sante, *New York Review of Books*

"No one can turn a phrase like Westlake."

—*Detroit News and Free Press*

The Rare Coin Score

Parker Novels By Richard Stark

The Hunter [Payback]
The Man with the Getaway Face
The Outfit
The Mourner
The Score
The Jugger
The Seventh
The Handle
The Rare Coin Score
The Green Eagle Score
The Black Ice Score
The Sour Lemon Score
Deadly Edge
Slayground
Plunder Squad
Butcher's Moon
Comeback
Backflash
Flashfire
Firebreak
Breakout
Nobody Runs Forever
Ask the Parrot
Dirty Money

The Rare Coin Score

RICHARD STARK

With a New Foreword by Luc Sante

The University of Chicago Press

The University of Chicago Press, Chicago, 60637

University of Chicago Press edition 2009

Printed in the United States of America

18 17 16 15 14 13 12 11 10 09   1 2 3 4 5

ISBN-13: 978-0-226-77107-6 (paper)
ISBN-10: 0-226-77107-5 (paper)

Library of Congress Cataloging-in-Publication Data

Stark, Richard, 1933–2008.
The rare coin score / Richard Stark ; with a new foreword by Luc Sante.
p. cm.
Summary: Parker makes the mistake of letting an amateur in on the score, and one of them is a pretty woman named Claire.
ISBN-13: 978-0-226-77107-6 (pbk. : alk. paper)
ISBN-10: 0-226-77107-5 (pbk. : alk. paper) 1. Parker (Fictitious character)—Fiction. 2. Criminals—Fiction. I. Sante, Luc. II. Title.
PS3573.E9R37 2009
813'.54—dc22

2009006774

♾ The paper used in this publication meets the minimum requirements of the American National Standard for Information Sciences—Permanence of Paper for Printed Library Materials, ANSI Z39.48-1992.

Foreword

THE PARKER novels by Richard Stark are a singularly long-lasting literary franchise, established in 1962 and pursued to the present, albeit with a twenty-three-year hiatus in the middle. In other ways, too, they are a unique proposition. When I read my first Parker novel—picked up at random, and in French translation, no less—I was a teenager, and hadn't read much crime fiction beyond Sherlock Holmes and Agatha Christie. I was stunned by the book, by its power and economy and the fact that it blithely dispensed with moral judgment, and of course I wanted more. Not only did I want more Parker and more Stark, I also imagined that I had stumbled upon a particularly brilliant specimen of a thriving genre. But I was wrong. There is no such genre.

To be sure, there are plenty of tight, harsh crime novels, beginning with Dashiell Hammett's *Red Harvest*, and there is a substantial body of books written from the point of view of the criminal, ranging from the tortured cries of Jim Thompson and David Goodis to the mordantly analytical *romans durs* by Georges Simenon. There are quite a few caper novels, including the comic misadventures Parker's creator writes under his real name, Donald Westlake, and the works of a whole troop of French writers not well known in this country: José Giovanni, Albert Simonin, San-Antonio. The lean, efficient Giovanni in particular has points in common with Stark (Anglophones can best approach him through movie adaptations: Jean-Pierre Melville's *Le deuxième souffle*, Claude Sautet's *Classe tous risques*), but with the key difference that Giovanni is an unabashed romantic.

Stark is not a romantic, or at least not within the first six feet down from the surface. Westlake has said that he meant the books to be about "a workman at work," which they are, and that is why they have so few useful parallels, why they are virtually a genre unto themselves. Process and mechanics and troubleshooting dominate the books, determine their plots, underlie their aesthetics and their moral structure. A great many of the editions down through the years have prominently featured a blurb from Anthony Boucher: "Nobody tops Stark in his objective portrayal of a world of total amorality." That is true as far as it goes—it is never suggested in the novels that robbing payrolls or shooting people who present liabilities are anything more than business practices—but Boucher overlooked the fact that Parker maintains his own very lively set of moral prerogatives. Parker abhors waste, sloth, frivolity, inconstancy, double-dealing, and reckless endangerment as much as any Puritan. He hates dishonesty with a passion, although you and he may differ on its terms. He is a craftsman who takes pride in his work.

Parker is in fact a bit like the ideal author of a crime-fiction series: solid, dependable, attentive to every nuance and detail. He is annoyed by small talk and gets straight to the point in every instance, using no more than the necessary number of words to achieve his aim. He eschews shortcuts, although he can make difficult processes look easy, and he is free of any trace of sentiment, although he knows that while planning and method and structure are crucial, character is even more important. As brilliant as he is as a strategist, he is nothing short of phenomenal at instantly grasping character. This means that he sometimes sounds more like a fictional detective than a crook, but mostly he sounds like a writer. In order to decide which path the double-crosser he is pursuing is most likely to have taken, or which member of the string is most likely to double-cross, or the odds on a reasonable-sounding job that has just been proposed to him by someone with shaky credentials, he has to get all the way under the skin of the party in question. He is an exceptionally intelligent freelancer in a risky profession who takes on difficult jobs hoping for a payoff large enough to hold off the next job for as long as possible. He even has an agent (Joe Sheer succeeded by Handy McKay). Then again he is seen—by other characters as well as readers—as lacking in emotion, let alone sympathy, a thug whose sole motivation is self-interest.

And no wonder: Parker is a big, tough man with cold eyes. "His hands looked like they'd been molded of brown clay by a sculptor who thought big and liked veins"; the sentence appears like a Homeric epithet somewhere in an early chapter of most of the books. He might just possibly pass for a businessman, provided the business is something like used cars or jukeboxes. He doesn't drink much, doesn't gamble, doesn't read, likes to sit in the dark, thinking, or else in front of the television, not watching but employing it as an aid to concentration. Crude and antisocial at the start of the series, he actually evolves considerably over its course. Claire, whom he meets in *The Rare Coin Score,* seems to have a lot to do with this—by *Deadly Edge* they actually have a house together. And Alan Grofield, first encountered in *The Score* and recurring in *The Handle,* among other titles, twice in the series becomes the recipient of what can only be called acts of kindness from Parker, however much Stark equivocates on this point, insisting that they merely reflect professional ethics or some such.

Parker is a sort of supercriminal—not at all like those European master criminals, such as Fantômas and Dr. Mabuse, but a very American freebooter, able to outmaneuver the Mob, the CIA, and whatever other forces come at him. For all that he lives on the other side of the law, he bears a certain resemblance to popular avengers of the 1960s and '70s, Dirty Harry or Charles Bronson's character in *Death Wish.* He is a bit of a fanatic, and even though we are repeatedly told how sybaritic his off duty resort-hotel lifestyle is, it remains hard to picture, since he is such an ascetic in the course of the stories. He is so utterly consumed by the requirements of his profession that everything extraneous to it is suppressed when he's on, and we are not privy to his time off, except for narrow vignettes in which he is glimpsed having sex or, once, swimming. But then, writers are writing even when they're not writing, aren't they?

After *The Hunter,* all the remaining titles concern jobs gone wrong, which seems to be the case for most of Parker's jobs, barring the occasional fleeting allusion to smoother operations in the past. *The Seventh* is, naturally, the seventh book in the series, as well as a reference to the split from the take in a stadium job. The actual operation is successful; the problem is what occurs afterward. It represents the very rare incursion, for the Parker series, of a thriller staple: the crazed gunman. Along with *The Rare Coin Score*, it is one of Stark's always very-pointed explorations of group dynamics. *The Handle,* with its private gambling island, ex-Nazi villain, and international intrigue, is (like *The Mourner* and *The Black Ice Score*) a nod to the espionage craze of the 1960s, when authors of thrillers could not afford to ignore James Bond. If *The Seventh* is primarily aftermath, *The Handle* is largely preamble. In *The Rare Coin Score* (the first of four such titles, succeeded by *Green Eagle, Black Ice, and Sour Lemon*) the culprit is an amateur, a coin dealer whose arrested development is so convincingly depicted the reader can virtually hear his voice squeak. Sharp characterizations abound in this one—its plot turns entirely on character flaws of various sizes.

The Parker books are all engines, machines that start up with varying levels of difficulty, then run through a process until they are done, although subject to different sorts of interference. The heists depicted are only part of this process—sometimes they are even peripheral to it. Parker is the mechanic who runs the machine and attempts to keep it oiled and on course. The interference is always caused by personalities—by the greed, incompetence, treachery, duplicity, or insanity of individuals concerned, although this plays out in a variety of ways, depending on whether it affects the job at beginning, middle, or end, and whether it occurs as a single dramatic action, a domino sequence of contingencies, or a gradually fraying rope. The beauty of the machine is that not only does it allow for the usual suspense, but it also maximizes the effectiveness of its opposite: the satisfaction of inevitability. Some Parker novels are fantastically intricate clockwork mechanisms (*The Hunter, The Outfit,* the seemingly unstoppable *Slayground,* the epic *Butcher's Moon*), while others hurtle along as successions of breakdowns (the aptly acidic *The Sour Lemon Score,* the almost sadistically frustrating *Plunder Squad*). Like all machines but unlike lesser thrillers the novels have numerous moving parts, and the more the better—more people, more subplots, more businesslike detail, more glimpses of marginal lives. Stark's momentum is such that the more matter he throws into the hopper the faster the gears turn. The books are machines that all but read themselves. You can read the entire series and not once have to invest in a bookmark.

Luc Sante
December 2008

The Rare Coin Score

PART ONE

1

PARKER SPENT two weeks on the white sand beach at Biloxi, and on a white sandy bitch named Belle, but he was restless, and one day without thinking about it he checked out and sent a forwarding address to Handy McKay and moved on to New Orleans. He took a room in a downtown motel and connected with a girl folk singer the first night, but all she did was complain how her manager was lousing up her career, so three days later he ditched her and took up with a Bourbon Street stripper instead.

But he kept being restless. After a week, he split with the stripper and went down to the waterfront one night and kept walking around till two guys jumped him for his shoes. When he noticed he was prolonging the fight for the pleasure of it, he got disgusted and finished them off and went back to the hotel and packed. He sent the new address to Handy McKay and took an early-morning plane to Las Vegas.

Vegas was a bad idea, because he wasn't a gambler. He was restless all the time and couldn't seem to stop going after women. One afternoon and evening he had three of them, and called the third one by the first one's name. She stuck around anyway, but it told him he was getting too distracted, so the next day he took a plane to San Diego and put down a week's rent on a beach cottage south of the city, to be alone for a while. He sent out the new address, as usual, and lay down on the beach in the sun.

He couldn't stop thinking about women, but he knew what that meant; it was just his nerves wanting him to go to work again. But it was stupid to think about work now, and Parker didn't like to be stupid. He still had more than enough left from the last job, and a lot salted away in different places around the country, so there was no need yet to take on something new. When work got to be its own reason for happening, that was trouble.

Still, he lay alone and restless on the beach, his eyes closed against the sun while his mind ran around and around about women, and his nerves didn't ever want to quiet down. He told himself he'd stay out his week's rent, no matter what, and not go after any women while he was here. He spent a lot of time in the cold ocean water, and in the evenings sat and looked at the fuzzy television set that had come with the cottage, and all the time the nerves kept jumping just below the surface of his skin.

The fifth day, he walked down the beach and picked up a thirty-year-old divorcée from somewhere in Texas, who'd come out to the Coast because she'd been hearing this was where the action was and she wanted to find out what the action was before it was too late to do anything about it. He took her back to the cottage and broke the seal on a pint of Scotch and gave her an hour of talk so she wouldn't feel like a pickup. The hour was just about up when the phone rang.

It was Handy McKay's voice, spinning along the wire all the way from Presque Isle, Maine, saying, "Hello. You busy?"

"Hold on," Parker said, and turned toward the divorcée with a smile different from any smile she'd seen on him before this, and he told her, "Go home."

2

PARKER LAY in the dark on his hotel-room bed and waited to be contacted. Lying there, he looked like a machine not yet turned on. He was thinking about nothing; his nerves were still.

When the knock sounded at the door, he got up and walked over and switched on the light, because he knew most people thought it strange when somebody lay waiting in the dark. Then he opened the door and there was a woman standing there, which he hadn't expected. She was tall and slender and self-possessed, with the face and figure of a fashion model, very remote and cool. She said, "Mr. Lynch?"

That was the name he was using here, but he said, "You sure this is the room you want?"

"May I come in?"

"Maybe you want some other Lynch," he said.

Her mouth showed impatience. "I really am from Billy Lebatard, Mr. Lynch," she said. "And it would be better if we didn't talk in the hall."

He shook his head. "Try another name."

"You mean Lempke?"

"That's the one," he said, and stepped back from the doorway, motioning her into the room.

She came in, still unruffled and self-possessed, saying, "Is all that caution really needed at this point?"

He shut the door. "I didn't expect a woman," he said.

"Oh? Why not?"

"It's unprofessional."

She smiled slightly, with one side of her mouth. "It doesn't sound like a very rewarding profession."

Parker had no patience with pointless games. He shrugged and said, "What happens now?"

"I drive you to the meeting."

"What meeting?"

She allowed herself to be surprised. "The meeting you're here for. Did you think you'd just do it without any plan at all?"

Parker hadn't yet decided whether or not he would do this one, but there was no point saying so; she was just a chauffeur. Besides, if she was any indication of how things would be handled here, he'd be out of it anyway.

But he would go to this first meeting, just to see the lay of the land. At the worst it was a chance to renew a couple of old touches. It was tough in this line of work to keep current with old friends, but the only way to build the right string for any job was to know who was available.

So he slipped into his suit jacket, pocketed his room key, and said, "All right, we'll go have a meeting."

They left the hotel and she led him around onto Washington Street and over to a green Buick station wagon, where she said, "Do you want to drive?"

"You know this town?"

She shrugged and made a face and said, "Fairly well." As though what she meant was, more than I like.

"Then you drive," he said, and walked around to the passenger side and got in.

She looked after him in surprise, then opened the driver's door herself and slid in behind the wheel. She put the key in the ignition, but instead of starting the engine she sat back and began to study him, frowning to herself.

Parker waited, but she just kept sitting there and looking at him as though she was trying to read something written on the inside of his head, so after a while he said, "Okay, get it over with."

"I'd just like to know," she said.

"Ask."

"Are you just naturally rude, or are you trying to antagonize me for some reason?"

Parker shook his head. "All you do is drive the car."

"In other words, I don't matter."

"Right."

She nodded. "Fine by me," she said. "It just took me by surprise, that's all."

There was nothing to say to that, so Parker faced front and got out his cigarettes. He lit one for himself while she was starting the engine, and then sat back and watched Indianapolis slide by. It was a little after midnight of a Wednesday night and the streets were deserted. They were also very wide and very brightly lit, so it was like driving through a recently abandoned city, except that here and there neon lights flashed in the windows of closed drugstores and supermarkets. Parker watched all that emptiness outside the windshield, and it seemed to him this should be a good town for a late-night haul.

It was good to be thinking right again. His mind had snapped into shape two days ago, the instant he'd heard Handy McKay's voice on the telephone, and he'd been cold and solid and sound ever since.

The conversation had been brief, once the astonished and disgruntled divorcée had been gotten rid of. Handy said, "Ran into a pal of yours the other day. Lempke."

That was a good name. Parker hadn't worked with Lempke in years, but he remembered him as reliable. He said, "How is he these days?"

"Keeping busy. He wanted to look you up sometime."

"I'd like to see him."

"You could try a friend of his at the Barkley Hotel in Chicago."

Parker, understanding that the friend was Lempke himself under an alias, said, "Maybe I will. What's the name?"

"Moore. John Moore."

"Got it. You still retired?"

'Still and forever. Drop in sometime."

"I will," Parker said, knowing he wouldn't, and hung up.

The conversation with Lempke was even briefer. Not identifying himself, Parker said, "I was talking to Handy the other day. He said we might get together."

"Not me," said Lempke. "But a fella named Lynch might register at the Clayborn Hotel in Indianapolis on Wednesday. That might be something for you, if you're interested."

"Thanks for the tip," said Parker, and on Wednesday he'd arrived at the Clayborn Hotel in Indianapolis, registered under the name of Lynch, and waited.

Now the waiting was done. He was surprised to be met by a woman, but with Lempke in it the job could still be good. The name she'd dropped—Billy Lebatard—meant nothing to him, and was unlikely to be another name of Lempke's, since Lempke knew enough not to use his own initials on new names.

The woman drove at a fast and steady pace south-westward away from the center of town. The avenue narrowed, grew less brightly lit, more residential. There were no hills anywhere, nothing but flatness. Parker noticed the woman glance at him out of the corner of her eye as the cops went by.

What did she expect him to do? Flinch, put his hands over his face, jump from the car and start running, pull out a pistol and bang away?

He threw his cigarette out of the window, shut his eyes, and waited for the ride to stop.

3

ON A SIDE street in Mars Hill, southwest of the city proper, the woman made a right turn into a gravel driveway beside a small frame one-story house. There were few streetlights out here, and many trees, but Parker could see enough to know it was a rundown seedy neighborhood and that this house blended perfectly with the rest. There was no garage, and the front yard was bare brown earth except for a few weeds. There were lights in the windows of the house, but the shades were all drawn full down.

The woman said, unnecessarily, "Here we are," and switched off the engine.

Parker got out of the Buick and shut the door, then waited for the woman to let him know whether they were supposed to go to the front or the back. She took longer getting out, but finally was ready, and said, "This way."

The front. There was a narrow bare porch. The woman knocked on the glass of the door, which probably meant the bell didn't work.

The door opened and a pudgy kid was standing there. Or maybe not a kid. But short, and soft, and covered with baby fat. He wore a wrinkled white shirt open at the collar and bunched at the waist, and dark trousers with unmatching jacket, and black shoes, and large eyeglasses with black rims. He had thinning black hair, and a round white face, and soft hands with stubby fingers. He said, "Claire! And this must be Mr. Parker." His voice was high-pitched and weak, making Parker think of eunuchs.

The woman—Claire—stepped into the house, saying,

"Hello, Billy. His name is supposed to be Lynch." There was a resigned quality in her voice now that hadn't been present before, as though all her objections had long ago worn themselves out on the unlined brow of Billy.

"We're all friends here," Billy said, and laughed, and extended a soft hand toward Parker, saying, "I'm Billy Lebatard, this is my show. Lempke's told me a lot about you."

Parker stepped inside, ignored the outstretched hand, and pulled the door away from Billy's other hand, shutting it, saying, "Did he tell you I don't like to be framed in a lit doorway?"

Billy's smiling face went blank, but without losing the smile, which hung on like a leftover crescent moon. He looked over at Claire, who was half-turned away from him, looking through the archway into the living room, and he said, "Claire? Did I do something wrong?"

"Probably," she said wearily, not turning her head, and walked away into the living room.

Parker said, "Is Lempke here?"

"Well, certainly," said Billy, suddenly happy again. "We're all here, just waiting for you."

"Is that right?"

"Lempke tells me you're an idea man, an organizer. He tells me you're just the man we need for this job."

"Maybe. Where is he?"

"In the living room," Billy said eagerly. "We're all here in the living room." He moved off, urging Parker to move with him, not quite touching Parker's arm.

The living room was small and cramped and full of furniture. Two lamps and a ceiling light were all burning, making the room bright and garish and semi-hysterical. A shabby dining room, also brightly lit, was through an archway on the left. The ceiling was low, making the room seem even more crowded than it was.

Lempke was sitting on the overstuffed mohair sofa straight ahead, a can of beer in his hand. He looked much older than Parker remembered. A small, neat, spare man in his mid-fifties, he gave the impression of being scrubbed, like a child leaving home for the first day of school. When he smiled—as he did now, seeing Parker—he showed the smallest, neatest, whitest, falsest set of false teeth Parker had ever seen, and from the look of them Parker guessed that Lempke had been on the inside for a while since they'd last worked together. Those choppers looked like the kind of thing you might expect from a prison dentist.

Lempke got to his feet, extending his hand, saying, "Parker. Long time no see."

"Good to see you again, Lempke," Parker said, though it maybe wasn't true. If Lempke was fresh out of the house his judgment might not be trustworthy. He might be too hungry for a score, might be tempted to sign on somewhere even if the setup wasn't one hundred per cent right.

Lempke said, "I don't think you know Jack French," motioning at the man who'd been sitting next to him on the sofa.

"No, I don't."

French stood up as he was introduced, and Parker shook hands with him. He thought French looked all right; lean and rawboned and self-contained, maybe thirty-five, with level eyes and an expressionless face. French said, "Good to know you," and sat down again.

"Now we're all here," Billy was saying, beaming and rubbing his soft hands together.

Parker said to Lempke, "What's the pitch?"

But Lempke said, "Lebatard ought to tell you, it's his baby."

"Sit down, Mr. Parker," Billy said, happy and eager. "Take the comfortable chair there, I'll tell you all about it."

Flanking the television set opposite the sofa was a pair of mismatched armchairs, both with frayed backs and arms. Claire was sitting in one of these now, legs crossed, absorbed in a study of her stocking. Parker went to the other and sat down, liking this situation less and less. Billy Lebatard seemed to be running this operation, and Billy Lebatard was an obvious amateur and fool. Sweet jobs were occasionally fingered by amateurs and fools, but the odds weren't good. Feeling more and more that he'd been dealt a hand he should fold, Parker sat down and waited for the fool to tell him what it was all about.

Billy stood in the middle of the room, turning this way and that, trying to smile at everybody at once. "For the benefit of the two new men," he said, in his child's voice, "I'll start at the beginning. My name is Billy Lebatard, and by profession I'm a numismatist. A coin dealer. And stamps, some stamps, but mostly coins."

Jack French abruptly said, "How come you're heeled?"

That was nicely done. Parker set himself to back French's play, if called upon.

But Billy just looked flustered for a few seconds, and then looked down at himself, at the bulge under his jacket on the left side, and laughed sheepishly and said, "That's just habit. I didn't even think about that." He looked at French, grinning like a kid who's finally got to play with the big boys, and he said, "I carry valuable coins with me a lot. Sometimes sixty or seventy thousand dollars in the back of the station wagon."

French said, "You got coins on you now?"

"I'll put it away if you want me to," Billy said. "But aren't you all—?" He gestured vaguely, and looked around at Parker, and then at Lempke.

It was Lempke who answered him. "None of us is carrying, Billy," he said. He spoke patiently, like a sad father explaining something obvious to the son who hasn't worked out. "When you're meeting friends," he said, "there's no need to be armed."

"I didn't real—I'll put it away right away. I'm sorry, I'm really sorry." He laughed again, nervous and sheepish, saying, "You know how it is, you get into the habit, you don't even know you're—" He trailed on out of the room, babbling, smiling at everybody, his white forehead gleaming in the light.

When Billy was finally out of the room, French looked over at Parker and said, "A C note it's pearl-handled."

"Chrome," said Claire.

Parker looked at Claire, but she was still studying her stocking. She didn't figure in this setup, and what didn't figure Parker didn't like. Unless Billy Lebatard, aside from being an amateur and a fool, was also a masochist, there just wasn't any explanation for Claire. The weary contempt she felt for him and all his works shone out like the green on a rotten orange.

Lempke said, "Give him a chance, Jack. He's got personality problems, but the setup's a sweet one."

"Maybe," said French. He sounded as though he didn't

believe it.

Parker said to Lempke, "Does he just finger, or does he want in?"

French added, "With his chrome-handled .25."

Claire laughed briefly, shaking her head, and Lempke said, "He'll be in on it, he has to be. But not with the gun."

Billy Lebatard came back in then, and he'd removed the suit jacket as well. His white shirt was soaking wet across the back and under the arms; he'd given up a lot of comfort in order to impress himself by wearing his coat and pistol. He said, "All set now," and smiled foolishly at everybody.

Parker said, "Lempke, tell us the story."

Lempke made an awkward gesture, saying, "Billy ought to—"

"You tell it," Parker said.

Billy laughed brightly and said, "Maybe that's best. I'll just sit over here and listen." There was a kitchen chair against a side wall, far from where Claire was sitting, and this was where Billy settled himself, sitting lumpishly with his legs apart and his hands resting on his thighs.

Lempke said, "It's coins, Parker. Billy fingers and does the financing, and when it's done he gives us fifty per cent on the take."

Parker shook his head. "Bad," he said.

"Why?"

"There's never enough profit in those. You hit a coin dealer, he's got goods worth maybe forty, fifty grand. That's twenty-five for us. Split three ways, it isn't enough."

French said, "I did one of those once, when I was hungry. Me and a fella named Stimson. A coin dealer fingered it, same as here. We followed this other dealer away from one of those conventions they have, hijacked him on the Turnpike. We split a lousy eighteen grand between us, and Stimson got a bullet in his leg."

"But this isn't just one dealer," Lempke said. "This time it's a whole convention." He turned to Parker, saying, "You know anything about these coin conventions?"

"No."

"They're not a regular convention like doctors or anything

like that. It's kind of like a sale. A whole lot of dealers get together, and they rent a hotel ballroom or someplace like that, and set out their stuff over a whole weekend, so the local hobby types can come in and buy."

Billy said, "The local coin club is host. They arrange for the hotel and the banquet and displays and tours and everything."

Lempke said, "You get a good-size coin convention, there's sometimes three million dollars in coins there."

Parker said, "How do we get at it?"

"Let Billy tell you that."

Billy leaned forward eagerly, his hands pressing down on his thighs, and said, "The dealers set up Friday morning in the bourse room, and most of them come to town the night before. So there's a special room set aside, they call it the security room, and everybody checks their stock in there on Thursday night for safekeeping. Maybe three-quarters of the dealers have their stock in the security room Thursday night."

Lempke said, "Billy's idea is, we break into the security room late Thursday night, clean it out. He figures close to two million dollars."

French said, "Our piece is a million."

"Close to it," Lempke agreed. "That's what Billy figures."

"And he pays us when?"

"As I liquidate the stock," Billy said, and laughed, saying, "If I had a million dollars, I wouldn't need to do any of this."

"I figured it was like that," said French. He got to his feet. "Nothing against you, Lempke, but I don't work on IOU's."

Lempke said, "Jack, this is rock solid. I know Billy, I can vouch for him."

Parker said, "Lempke, when did you get out?"

Lempke looked at him in surprise. "Where'd you hear about that?"

"From you. You're too hungry to be smart."

"Parker, you got to listen to the rest of this."

"No, I don't." Parker got to his feet, and said to French, "I'll take a cab with you."

When they left, Lempke was looking after them with a pleading expression on his face, Billy was smiling in bewilderment at Lempke, and Claire was wearily studying her fingernails.

4

THEY WALKED six blocks before they found a bar where they could call for a cab. Along the way, they found out there were half a dozen people they knew in common. Because they didn't know each other yet, they avoided mention of any specific jobs either of them had been on.

As they walked along, French said, "I'm sorry that wasn't any good. I could use a job. I'm dipping into my stake. You don't know anything else happening, do you?"

"No," said Parker. "But I'd like to."

"If you hear of anything—"

"Sure," said Parker. "The way to get in touch with me is through a fella named Handy McKay in Presque Isle, Maine."

"I think I met him once," said French. "He's in the business, too, isn't he?"

"Retired a couple years ago. The two of us got shot up on something that went sour."

"It takes a smart man to retire," said French. "My man is Solly Hinkle, San Antonio. Tell him the Frenchman."

"Right."

They went into the bar, called a cab, and sat at a booth with drinks till it came. Neither of them was much of a talker, so they sat in silence, hands around their drinks. Three locals at the bar were telling each other about Willie Sutton, deciding he was a genius and they just don't make them anymore like that these days.

The cab got there about ten minutes later. They got in and French told the driver, "Union Station." Then, to Parker, "You've got to go back to your hotel, don't you?"

"Right. The Clayborn."

The cab started up, and Parker sat and tried to decide where to go tomorrow. There were unlikely to be any more planes out tonight, so he'd have to stay over.

If French was traveling by train, he must be really close to the edge of his cash. He'd said he was going into his stake, but he hadn't said how long that had been going on. To be that tight, and yet to turn down a job that fast, meant a good man. Parker filed the contact's name and address in his head for some other time.

French got out at Union Station, and from there it was a quick drive up Illinois Street to the Clayborn. There shouldn't have been any messages at the desk, and there weren't any, but he checked anyway. He thought about calling Handy, but he didn't have anything to say to him yet, and if Handy had any other kind of news it could wait till morning.

Parker went on up to his room. He neither undressed nor turned on a light, but went over in the dark to his bed and lay down there on his back, looking up into the darkness.

There was no place he wanted to go, but he knew he wouldn't be getting to sleep until he'd made some sort of decision about tomorrow. He thought about going out again, looking for a woman, but at one o'clock on a Wednesday night in Indianapolis the prospects were probably very bad.

He thought about all the towns he knew, all the places he'd ever been, from Miami to Seattle, from San Diego to New York, and there was nothing good to be said about any of them.

He lay looking up into the darkness at the ceiling, and his nerves were starting to jump again.

5

WHOEVER WAS knocking at the door wouldn't quit, so after a while Parker got up and went to see who was there. He didn't turn the light on this time, because he didn't care about whoever this was.

Claire. She said, "I thought you were asleep. At the desk, they said you were in." She was looking at the darkness of the room behind him, and registering the fact that he was dressed.

Parker said, "Billy sent you to sex me back in. Tell him forget it."

She shook her head. "Billy doesn't send me anywhere," she said. "You've got the wrong idea about us."

"I don't have any ideas about you. Go home."

But she wouldn't. Pressing one hand against the door, she said, "Do you really think Billy's the one behind this idea? Do you really think he's got the brains to know what time it is?"

He shook his head. "It doesn't matter whose idea it is," he said. "It's still sour."

"It doesn't have to be, I know it doesn't. Let me in, let me talk to you."

"There's no point," he said, but he felt his restlessness winning out over logic. Not urging him to get back into Billy Lebatard's harebrained scheme, but just to spend some time with this woman; listen to her, bed her, fill an hour or so till he could sleep.

She sensed his indecision, but maybe not its cause, and pressed the point, leaning inward toward him, palm still pressed flat against the door. "Just let me talk to you for five minutes. Five minutes."

Abruptly he shrugged and stepped back and said, "Come in then."

She went past him into the darkened room, and he shut the door. In the dark her disembodied voice said, "Why don't you turn on a light?"

"I can concentrate this way," he said. "You just talk, I'll listen."

"I can't see anything," she complained.

He walked past her, knowing where the bed was, and stretched out on it. "You don't have to see," he said. "Just talk."

"Why do you have to pressure me like this?"

"You came here," he reminded her.

In the next silence he could hear her taking out her pride and looking at it and deciding it wasn't worth the gesture and putting it away in a box till some time when she could tie the score. When next she spoke, her voice was level and flat and emotionless: "Where do I find a chair?"

"To your left, and back."

She found it without stumbling into anything, and waited till she was seated before lighting a match and putting it to a cigarette. Looking at her in the small yellow light, he felt the first surge of specific desire for this individual woman. He looked up at the ceiling and watched the shadows there until the match went out.

She said, "It's nine days from now, in this hotel."

"They must have scraped out Lempke's skull, up there in the big house."

"Why?"

"He's forgotten everything he ever knew. You and Lebatard, you're amateurs, but Lempke should know."

"What should he know?"

"Number one, you don't meet in the town where you're going to make the hit. Number two, you don't stay in the hotel where you're going to make the hit. Number three, you don't take a job on consignment; we're in the wrong business to take your Billy to court if he doesn't pay."

"You can kill him."

"How much does that make me?"

"I mean, Billy won't try to cheat you because he's afraid of you. All of you. He knows if he doesn't pay, you'll kill him."

There was nothing to say to that, so Parker simply closed his eyes and waited.

After a minute, she said, "I know there's a certain amount of risk in this, but there's risk in it every time, isn't there?"

When she kept waiting for an answer, he said, "Don't put those silences in, I'll go to sleep."

"Well, isn't there risk all the time?"

"You're here to tell me, not ask me."

"All right. My husband was a pilot with Transocean. Billy is his sister's husband's brother. When my husband was killed, Billy started hanging around. I told him no, but he keeps saying he just wants to be my friend, he wants to help me. I need a lot of money, and I told him so, and he said he'd get it for me."

Parker said, "You told him you wouldn't give, but you would sell."

"If he wants to take it that way, it isn't my fault. He said he wanted to help, and I knew what I needed, and I told him. He's done this kind of thing before, you know. Hire people to steal from other coin dealers. Except for the really rare ones, coins are absolutely untraceable."

"You need more than he can get from a simple dealer heist?"

"I need seventy thousand dollars."

"Seventy grand. That's friendship."

"What I do is my business."

"Right. And what I don't do is mine."

There was a pause, and then she said, in a softer voice, "I'm sorry. I know how it sounds, but I do what I have to do."

"Take off your clothes."

The silence this time had sharp edges on it, and so did her voice when she said, "That's your price?"

"Yes."

"Then I'll get someone else."

He let her reach the door, and then he said, "Your line was, 'I do what I have to do.' But that's a lie, you wear your pride like it'd keep the cold out. What you mean is, you despise Lebatard and don't care what you do to him."

She shut the door again, bringing back the darkness. She

said, "What's wrong with that?"

"Another rule," he said. "Don't work with anyone you can't trust or don't respect."

"You have too many rules," she said.

"I haven't been inside. Lempke has."

"What would you have done if I had taken my clothes off?"

"Taken you to bed and left in the morning."

"Maybe it isn't pride," she said. "Maybe I'm just smart."

Parker laughed and sat up. "No more life story," he said. "Tell me the caper."

6

"THIS WILL be the bourse room," she said. "There'll be tables around the walls and two ranks of tables down the middle of the room, with one aisle going all the way around."

They were in the ballroom on the hotel mezzanine. It hadn't been used for anything tonight, and was open and empty, a long rectangular room with tall windows down at the far left end. A bluish-white streetlight gleamed in on the bare wood floor, making the place look like a basketball court in off-season. The wall opposite the doors was covered from end to end in maroon plush drapes, and the wall at the right bore a large historical mural, heavy with Indians.

"Down here," she said, and led the way to the left. Down in the far corner, near the windows, was a small inconspicuous door in the long wall. Opening it, she said, "This will be the security room. Where the dealers will keep everything Thursday night."

It was a small bare room, empty except for a cream telephone sitting on the floor. There was one window, through which the streetlight angularly shone. Looking out, Parker saw the hotel marquee down to his left, and the wide empty street outside.

"There should be a hundred dealers at this one," Claire said. "Seventy or eighty will get in Thursday night and check their stock in here."

"When's the convention over?"

"Sunday night."

"What do they do with their goods Friday and Saturday?"

She pointed at the ballroom. "They leave everything on the tables. There's Pinkerton guards here the whole time. There'll be one in this room, too."

There was a closed door in the wall opposite the window. Parker unlocked it, opened it slowly, saw there was no one in sight on the mezzanine, and stepped through to look around.

The mezzanine was constructed around a large rectangular opening overlooking the lobby, surrounded by a wide walkway with ornamental railing. To Parker's left was the double-doored ballroom entrance he and Claire had used. To the right, one-quarter around the walkway, were the elevators, with the staircase just beyond.

Parker stepped back into the room—a sign over the door said LAKE ROOM—relocked the door, and went over to take down the extension number of the telephone on the floor: one-nine-five. Then he turned to Claire, saying, "What else?"

"We'll go back outside."

They went through the ballroom again and back out to the walkway. Pointing across it, to the left of the elevators, she said, "The display room will be over there. Tables with special displays of sets of coins and paper money. But there's no use taking any of that, most of it is too readily identifiable."

Parker said, "So what we want is over here. Ballroom—what did you call it?"

"Bourse room."

"Right. Bourse room and security room." Parker looked thoughtfully around and said, "What about the Pinkerton men? Where are they stationed?"

"I don't know. We'd have to wait and see."

Parker grimaced. "All right, let's go back upstairs."

"Will you do it?"

"I don't know yet. I've still got questions."

"You ought to ask Billy, he knows more than I do."

"We'll see. Come on."

They walked around to the elevator, where she said, "You don't like it very much, do you?"

He didn't, but he said, "I don't see it yet, that's all. Maybe I'll never see it, I don't know."

The elevator came and they got aboard. She said, "But there's all that money there, all in one place."

"How much stock do these guys carry? A suitcase each?"

"Oh, at least," she said. "Most of them will have more than that. Two or three carrying cases."

The elevator reached seven. They walked down the hall, Parker saying, "Figure two suitcases a man. Full of coins. They'll be heavy, figure a rough guess, maybe fifty pounds each."

"Oh," she said. "That's a lot, isn't it?"

"A hundred fifty suitcases," he said, unlocking his door. They went in and he switched on the ceiling light.

Claire said, in a small voice, "Seventy-five hundred pounds."

"Round it off," Parker said. "Four tons. It's your idea to get three or four guys together and heist four tons of luggage."

"There's a way," she said, trying to sound as though she believed it. "There's a way to do anything, if you look for it."

"Sing that," he said.

"Damn it," she flared, "you're supposed to be the professional, why don't you think of something?"

"I have." He went over to the bed and stretched out on his back, hands behind his head.

"You have? What?"

"We stay away from the security room. We hit the bourse room late Saturday night."

"How?"

"I don't know yet. Maybe there's no job in it at all, but if there is one it's in the bourse room Saturday night."

"But everything's all unpacked then," she said.

"Good. We can pick and choose, just take the best stuff."

She was half-smiling, half-doubtful, hopeful, uncertain. She said, "Do you really suppose it can be done that way?"

"I don't know. I'll have to ask Lebatard some questions. Phone him now and tell him we'll see him in the morning."

She started to turn toward the phone, then looked back, saying, "In the morning?"

"It's up to you," he said.

"And if I say no, the deal's off?"

"Wrong. If you say no, you leave now and come back for me in the morning."

She seemed to consider, standing there near the phone. "That would be a lot of extra driving, wouldn't it?"

He got off the bed and reached for her. A while later she made the call.

7

"IT WON'T work that way," said Billy.

They were all in the backyard, at about ten-thirty in the morning. There was a small stone fireplace at the rear of the yard, at which Billy was cooking hamburgers. The wood he'd used wasn't completely dry, and was smoking badly.

Lempke was sitting on the bottom step of the back stoop, a beer can in his hand. He was wearing an old straw hat, and squinting against the sun. Claire, in blue slacks and white top, was sitting in a ribbed lawn chair, the only piece of furniture back there. Parker, restless and intent, was prowling around the scruffy yard like a panther in an outdoor enclosure at the zoo.

Parker said, "What's the problem? Why won't it work?"

"You take valuable coins," Billy said, gesturing with the spatula, "you just drop a lot of them in a canvas sack, carry them off someplace, dump them out on a table, you know what you've done?"

Parker said, "Tell me."

"You've lowered their value," Billy told him, "by maybe twenty-five per cent. Coins are more delicate than you might think. They rub together, knock together, the value goes right down. You go from unc to VF just like that."

"Billy," Claire said wearily, "they don't know those terms."

"I've got the idea," Parker said. "The point is, we've got to pack them up, right?"

"Time, Parker," Lempke said. "Time, time." Having had an extra night to think things over, Lempke had turned pessimistic and was now being discouraged and gloomy about the whole project.

Parker said, "It all depends." He turned back to Billy. "You say there'll be a hundred dealers there."

"About that. Maybe a few more, a few less."

"You don't want everything they've got."

"Not a bit," said Billy. "Some of the coins are too rare, I wouldn't dare to try to sell them without being able to show where I got them."

"And some," Parker suggested, "aren't worth enough to take."

"Foreign coins," Claire said.

"That's right," said Billy. "We don't want foreign coins, except maybe Canadian and Mexican. Mostly American we want."

Parker said, "So what's that cut it to? Half of the stuff there?"

"Oh, less than that." Billy thought, squinting in the smoke from his fire. "Maybe a third," he said. "Maybe only a quarter."

Lempke said, "Your burgers are burnin' up."

"Oh!"

Parker watched Billy, his head down in the smoke, turning his hamburgers. When he was done, Parker said, "How long would it take to pack up one dealer's stock?"

"How long?" Billy moved away from the smoke, waving the spatula in front of his face to clear the air. "I can do mine," he said, "I can do mine in, oh, three minutes."

"About thirty dealers. An hour and a half. Figure two hours, to be on the safe side."

"That's too much time," said Lempke. "In and out, that's the only way, Parker, you know that yourself. You hang around, hang around, you're asking for the collar."

Parker didn't bother answering him this time. He prowled around the yard, thinking it out, trying to see if there was a way to do it. More to himself than the others, he said, "Have to work a switch on the Pinkertons. One for one, one for one. Too many men."

Lempke said, "Parker, it isn't in the hand. You were right last night, you knew what you were talking about." He threw his empty beer can away across the lawn, and Billy looked pained.

"Maybe. Maybe." Parker wasn't as set on this job as Lempke

and the others thought; it was still merely just a way to occupy his mind for a while, an exercise, a playing around with professional theory.

Claire said to Lempke, "There's a way. And he'll find it."

Lempke looked from Parker to Claire and back again, then shrugged elaborately and got to his feet and went into the house for more beer.

Parker went over to Billy and said, "That means you're in it all the way, you know. Not just the fence, but inside. There for the heist. We need you to point out which ones we take."

Billy was plainly feeling both excitement and terror, trying unsuccessfully to hide both. "I'm willing," he said. "It's worth a lot to me, too, after all." He cast a quick glance toward Claire, then tried to look as though he hadn't.

"Two things," Parker told him. "One, you do what you're told. Two, you leave your bazooka home."

"But won't I—"

"No, you won't. Leave it home."

"If you say so," Billy said, looking troubled.

Lempke came back out onto the stoop, carrying a fresh can of beer, and called across the lawn, "Parker, how you going to do this thing?"

"I don't know yet," Parker said, and started toward the driveway, saying, "Claire, come on."

In surprise, Billy said, "Where are you going?"

"Find a way to make it happen," Parker said.

"Now? But what about the hamburgers?"

Parker didn't bother to answer him, but Claire said, as they walked around the corner of the house, "Eat them yourself."

8

"I MUST BE a masochist," Claire said. She was sitting up in bed, knees up, arms wrapped around her legs.

Parker, lying beside her, said, "I hadn't noticed."

She gave him a quick smile, then looked away again saying, "I'm always attracted to men who are about to get killed."

"Not always," said Parker. "Light me a cigarette."

"What, not you? You're the worst of them all." She took the cigarettes and matches from the night table, lit two cigarettes and gave him one. "The first boy I ever—ever went around with, drove in stock car races every weekend. His left leg was all scars from an accident."

Parker said, "Ashtray."

She put it on the sheet between them. "But all the others just tempted fate," she said. "You tempt fate and fight society at the same time."

"Wrong. I don't tempt anybody. I don't fight anybody. I walk where it looks safe. If it doesn't look safe, I don't walk."

"This time?"

He reached a hand up and stroked the long line of her back. "I haven't made up my mind yet."

"You'll do it," she said. "I know your type. You talk safety, but when you smell the right kind of danger you're off like a bloodhound."

She was describing a tendency in him that he'd been fighting all his life, and that he thought of as being under control. Also, it irritated him to be read that easily. With an abrupt movement, he got up from the bed, saying, "I've still got to look around, while it's light."

"Don't get mad at me," she said. "You were this way long before I came along."

Parker looked at her and said, "You talk yourself out of a lot of things, don't you?"

For just a second she looked stricken, but immediately got control again. "All right," she said, and shrugged. "We'll go look around."

They dressed and went down to the mezzanine for another look at the ballroom. Workmen in white overalls were in here now, standing on tall spindly ladders, putting up pink and white bunting across the ceiling.

Parker nodded at the wall opposite, the one covered in maroon plush. "What's on the other side of that?"

"I don't know. A wall."

"Past the wall."

"I really don't know."

"Wait here."

He walked through trailing streamers of pink and white to the maroon drapes, found a break in them, pushed them aside, and found a set of French doors with mirrored squares of glass. He looked at his silvered reflection, grim and intent, and beyond him Claire, standing across the room like a woman at an airport who knows it is impossible she will not be met.

He tried the wall at two other points, and it was all the same. The entire wall behind the drapes was lined in mirrored French doors. None of the doors had knobs or keyholes, and all seemed to be securely fastened to the wall.

Parker went back over to Claire and said, "Go stand by that window over there. I'm going out to the street. When I wave at you, come down and join me."

"All right. But what about—?" she motioned at the workmen.

"We're none of their business. Look at them, they don't pay any attention to us."

She made a quick and rueful smile, saying, "You're calmer about this than I am."

"I've been through it before."

He left, and went out to the street, turned right under the marquee, looked up, and saw Claire standing at the window. Just beyond that window was the end of the hotel, abutting another building, this one obviously much newer than the hotel. Between them, the hotel and the other building took up this entire block.

Parker waved, and Claire left the window.

The nearest window in the other building was about seven feet straight across from the one where Claire had been standing. This one had a cream-colored shade half drawn, was very wide, and had a small pot of African violets on the sill.

Claire came out of the hotel. When she joined him, Parker put his arm through hers and they walked down to the entrance to the next building, over which, in engraved letters, was written: MID-REGION INSURANCE BUILDING. A cornerstone down to the right said MCMXLVII.

Parker pointed at the date, saying, "What's the number? I'm no good at that stuff."

"Nineteen forty-seven."

They went in and up to the second floor. The door that seemed to lead in the direction they wanted was marked, DIABLO TOURS, The Caribbean Our Specialty. Parker said, "We're honeymooners, we don't know if we want Bermuda or Jamaica."

"All right."

They went into a smallish square room cluttered with travel posters and bisected by a chest-high counter. A fluttery woman in white peasant blouse, wide flowered skirt, hoop earrings, curly dull-brown hair and several charm bracelets was sitting at a messy desk on the other side of the counter. There was no pot of African violets on the windowsill, and a door on the farther wall apparently led to an inner office.

Under his breath, Parker said, "Get mad at her."

Claire nodded.

The fluttery woman got up from her desk, smiling as brightly as a bird, and came over to the counter, wondering if she could be of help. Parker gave her the honeymoon story, said they couldn't decide between Bermuda and Jamaica, and the woman assured them both islands were really very nice. She began pulling pamphlets and brochures out from under the counter, slapping them down in front of Parker and Claire, and then said, "And have you considered Puerto Rico? San Juan is really lovely, particularly if it's your first time in the Caribbean."

"That's the way you people always are," Claire said, suddenly harsh and bitchy. "Push us off to someplace where you get a payoff, never mind what *we* want."

The woman blushed scarlet. "Oh, my dear," she said, so flustered her hands were fidgeting in the brochures on the counter like pigeons after crumbs. "Oh, I hope you don't really think that of us, not really."

"Really," Claire said. "What are you people anyway but parasites? What good are you to anybody?"

"Really!" said the woman, suddenly stung. "No one asked you to come in here, after all."

"Now, just a minute," said Parker.

"If you don't want our services," the woman told him, obviously keeping herself under control with an effort, "that's entirely up to you. I wish you a pleasant voyage in any case."

"I don't like the way you talked to my fiancée," Parker said.

"Well, really. I mean really, after all, I *was* provoked."

Parker said, "I think I better talk to the manager."

"Miss Ross is not in at the moment."

Claire said, "That's what they always say."

Parker pointed at the door in the far wall. "That's the office, isn't it?"

The woman was getting flustered again. "I tell you, Miss Ross is out, she really is out."

"We'll see," Parker said. He went down to the end of the counter, raised the flap, and said to Claire, "Come on, Mary, we'll see about this."

"You can't come in here like that," the woman said, astonished and out of her depth. "You can't just—you can't—"

Parker, followed by Claire, went over to the door, opened it, and looked in at an empty office dominated by a large desk cluttered with papers. A pot of African violets was on the windowsill.

"You see," the woman was saying, vindicated. "She isn't there, she's out, just as I told you."

"We'll wait for her," Parker said, and went over to the brown leatherette sofa and sat down. Claire started to follow him, but he gave her a quick headshake and frowned toward the door.

She didn't get it at first, and simply stood there, near the doorway, looking at him and trying to figure it out.

"You can't wait in there," the woman was saying. "Really, this is too much. If you insist on waiting, there are quite comfortable chairs out here, on the *other side* of the counter."

"If my fiancée wants satisfaction," Parker said, "she'll get satisfaction."

Then Claire got it, and said, "Honey, let's forget it."

He frowned at her. "You sure?"

"We've got so much to do. And maybe I was a little hasty."

Parker acted like a man who doesn't want to show how relieved he is, shaking his head and looking around and grimacing, while the woman stood in the doorway trying to decide what expression she should have on her face to help these people choose to go away. Finally Parker said, reluctantly, "Well, if you say so," and got to his feet.

The woman obviously didn't trust the situation well enough to chance saying anything. She watched them in silence as they left the office, not responding when Claire waved and said, on her way out of the door, "Well, so long now."

Parker shut the door after them and said, "Bad. Always stay in character."

Grinning, Claire said, "I couldn't resist it."

"Next time try harder."

She immediately sobered, saying a terse, "Sorry."

They left the building and Parker walked back and forth on the sidewalk a while, studying the street and the building façades and the buildings across the way. Claire stood under the hotel marquee and watched.

When Parker was done with his look around, he and Claire went back into the hotel. In the lobby, he took out his wallet and handed her a five, saying, "Get me city and state maps and a pack of Luckies. Then call Lebatard from a booth, tell him we'll be out there at nine tonight to talk."

"Will do."

"And tell Lempke to come in here now, with a camera."

Watching him closely, she said, "Are we really going to do it?"

"And stop asking questions," he said.

9

BILLY LEBATARD was in the hallway outside Parker's room, looking pale and determined.

"You're an idiot," Parker said, and brushed past him to unlock the door.

"I want to talk to you," Billy said, trying to sound belligerent. All he sounded was overrehearsed. "Just the two of us," he said.

Parker opened the door and said, "Get in here before you tell the world we know each other."

Billy came in obediently, still parroting his prepared speech. "We've got to get things straight between us," he said.

"When this is all over," Parker said, shutting the door, "a couple of cops are going to come have a talk with you, they'll want to know who you came to see here today. You won't have an answer."

"Nobody I know saw me," said Billy defensively. He was thrown off-stride, and was standing in the middle of the room looking confused and worried, like a man listening to something important that's happening too far away for him to exactly make it out.

Parker said, "I don't care what happens to you, because they can't get to me through you. I'm just pointing things out. This is your town, you've got to live here. You want to go leaving trails, that's up to you."

"I won't have to live here forever. After this job, I can live anywhere. Maybe Majorca."

Parker nodded. "You're brilliant."

With an obvious effort, Billy got himself back on the track. "What I came here about—"

"I know what you came here about. There's only two things you can do about Claire. You can be the loser in her life, or you can cut loose. You can't have her, because she doesn't want you."

"That's for her to decide."

"Right." Parker went over and lay down on the bed.

Billy had lost his place in his script again. He gestured vaguely a bit, then blurted, "I want you to stay away from her. I know you're tough, I know you're—"

"Stop it, Billy." Parker closed his eyes, and spoke into the grayness: "Claire does what she wants to do. You coming here to get your nose broken doesn't change anything. She won't like you with blood on your face any more than she likes you now."

"I know you can beat me up," Billy said.

"You came here to make me beat you up," Parker told him. "Because the only thing you think you can hope for from Claire is pity." He opened his eyes and sat up and looked at Billy. "You know how you make pity? One jigger guilt, one jigger contempt. But Claire's got nothing to be guilty about over you."

"I'd rather this whole thing was called off, I'd rather—"

"Did you ever notice," Parker said, lying down again, putting his hands behind his head, looking up at the ceiling, "that funny scar she's got low on her stomach, a kind of crescent shape? How do you suppose she got that?"

There was nothing Billy could say to that. He was just coming to that understanding, and to the knowledge that the only move left to him was to rush at Parker and start hitting him with his fists, when the door opened and Claire came in, saying, "Billy isn't— Oh, here he is!"

Parker said, "Go out and walk around the halls and come back in."

Billy said, "No! You ought to hear this, too. I want—"

"That's all," Parker said. He got to his feet, saying, "It's off. The two of you get out of here."

Claire said, "Billy, if you gum things up. . ."

"All I wanted—"

"Go home, Billy," she said.

A sulky sullen child, Billy wagged his head back and forth, saying, "He has no right—"

"For the last time, Billy."

Reluctant, pouting, Billy scuffed out of the room.

Claire shut the door behind him and said to Parker, "It won't happen again. I promise."

Parker was at the window. Far below was the street, this room being on the same side as the ballroom. He stood looking down, trying to balance the pros and cons, trying to decide whether it was worth it to hang on a little longer.

She came over and stood just behind him. "I gave Lempke the message," she said. "He's on his way, with a Polaroid."

Parker kept looking out the window.

Tentatively she touched his arm. "I promise," she said.

There was nowhere else to go, nothing else to do. He shook himself and turned around. "Let's see the maps," he said.

PART TWO

1

WITH A camera slung around his neck, Lempke looked like a retired postal clerk, off on a world tour, who somewhere along the line has made a left turn when the rest of his charter group ("14 Days, 21 Countries!") made a right. He stood in the middle of Parker's hotel room, shoulders slumped as though the camera were dragging him down, seeming to be waiting for somebody to come along and find him. He said:

"You don't know what it's like on the inside, Parker, you never been."

Parker had done a little time in a prison farm once, but he knew it wasn't the same thing, so he let it ride, saying, "If you want clear of this, all you got to do is walk away."

Lempke's tiny false teeth gnawed his lower lip. "I need the money," he said. He looked at Claire, sitting over by the window and doing her nails. He shook his head, saying, "What I want is reassurance."

"About what?"

Lempke frowned, having trouble getting it out, and finally said, all in a rush, "That you aren't being influenced. This time."

Claire looked up from her nails, saying, "You mean me? I thought you knew Parker better than that."

"I don't want to go back inside, is all."

Parker said, "Then walk away."

"I can't."

Parker shook his head and walked around the room. "It's a bad string," he said. "One amateur, one scared old man."

"You never been in," Lempke said defensively.

"And I won't be after this one, either."

Claire abruptly said to Lempke, "Don't you have any grown children, anybody to take care of you?"

Lempke looked at her blankly, and Parker said, "That isn't how it works, Claire. Let it go."

She shrugged, and went back to her nails.

Parker said to Lempke, "You know you got to make up your mind now. If you stay, we don't talk about it any more."

Lempke moved his hands like a man feeling his way in the dark. "I'm troubled in my mind," he said. "There's so many problems."

"We'll do the easy one next year," Parker said.

"I know, I know." Lempke gnawed his lower lip some more, then abruptly made a violent shrugging motion that caused the camera to jump and bobble on his waist. "The hell," he said angrily. "The hell with it. You take the chances or you get out."

"Which is it?"

"In, in," Lempke said, still angry. "What am I, dead and buried? I walk around like I'm constipated." Then, to Claire, "Excuse the indelicacy."

She gestured with the nail-polish brush, accepting the apology and waving away all offense.

"All right," Parker said. "We want pictures."

"I'm your man." Lempke was standing straighter, looking determined, meeting Parker's eye; kidding himself.

Parker didn't push. He said, "The ballroom, all angles. Mezzanine, all angles. Lobby, both exits and stairs and elevators. Street, this sidewalk and the street itself, the front of the hotel with the ballroom windows, the building next door. And inside, next door, there's an outfit called Diablo Tours. We want the inner office, rear wall and window. You got color in that camera?"

"Sure. Nothing but the best."

"Good. I want pictures of an electric company repair truck, all angles. At work, if you can find one."

Lempke cocked his head to one side. "You already got it worked out?"

"Just a general idea. Better get started."

"Right!" Lempke went into a flurry of activity, moving his

hands and feet and head, demonstrating enthusiasm and capability, then all at once stopped everything and looked at Parker with gray eyes and said heavily, "Don't worry, I'll be all right."

"Good."

"Lempke's still down inside here," he said, patting his chest. "He'll come out when we need him."

"I know that," Parker lied.

"See you at Billy's tonight."

"Nine o'clock."

Lempke left, and Claire got to her feet, holding her hands out with fingers spread. "He shouldn't be like that, should he?" she said.

"No."

"Will he really be all right?"

"Probably not."

"What are you going to do?"

Parker shrugged. "Give him a chance to find out for himself."

"What if he doesn't?"

"He's right about one thing," Parker said. "He's still a pro down inside. If he should get out, sooner or later he'll know it, and he'll get out."

"But what if he doesn't?" she insisted.

"I said he will."

She looked at his face, and didn't ask again.

2

BILLY'S BASEMENT looked like an antique store in a blackout. The ceiling was low, made of hole-pocked white squares of soundproofing, with two fluorescent light fixtures with frosted glass. The floor was concrete, painted gray too long ago. The walls were lined with shelves, cabinets, drawers, narrow display cases, stacks. A large wooden table in the middle of the room contained a postage scale, stacks of manila envelopes, flat pieces of cardboard, a broad roll of brown wrapping paper, a sponge and a glass bowl, trays of stamps. A rolltop desk, shut and locked, was at the end near the stairs. Through a doorway at the other end could be seen the furnace.

When the four of them came downstairs, Lempke immediately went to the wooden chair by the mailing table and sat in it like a man waiting for death. In the fluorescent light his face had no color, except for faint grayness around the mouth and under the eyes. When he'd come back from taking his pictures, all the false strength had been gone. He'd said almost nothing since then.

Claire stayed in the shadow by the foot of the stairs, arms folded, as Parker followed Billy over to one of the display cases along the right-hand wall. Billy said, "This is how it'll be, all the coins out like this."

Parker looked in the display case and saw coins laid out in rows, each on a small square of orange paper. On each piece of paper, above and below the coin, was writing in pen: a price, and abbreviations.

Billy said, "I have some local customers, that's why I have these out like this. But most of my business is mail order."

Parker said, "Show me how this stuff is transported."

"That's over here."

Billy moved fussily away. Since the scene in the hotel room this afternoon, a change had come over him. He was all efficiency now, helpful and businesslike. He'd obviously decided his only course was to hold himself in until after the robbery, in hopes that Parker would then simply go away again and leave him with a clear path to Claire. How much of this he'd figured out for himself, and how much Claire had put into his head, Parker neither knew nor cared. Just so Billy stopped being a problem, that was all that mattered.

"Some people," Billy was saying, picking up a black suitcase and opening it on the glass top of one of the display cases, "carry their things this way. I do, too, when I'm going to have a lot. One of the bigger conventions."

The interior of the suitcase was all many-layered compartments. Billy demonstrated how coins were nested in these compartments, all of which were lined with felt. Parker, watching, saw it would be a long job for anyone not used to it, though Billy's hands moved with practiced speed, filling each compartment.

"All right," Parker said. "I got the idea. What's the other way?"

Billy immediately moved away from the suitcase, saying, "Some people, if they don't have too much, they might carry things this way." He took a small wooden cabinet down from a shelf, carried it over to the mailing table, put it down there. From the way he carried it, it was heavy. About sixteen inches high, six inches wide, a foot deep, it was all narrow drawers, with tiny round drawerpulls down the front, making it look like the control panel in a Victorian elevator.

"The advantage of this," Billy said, taking a drawer out and setting it down on the table, "is you don't really have to unpack. You just spread the drawers out on your table."

The drawers were lined with felt and full of coins. Parker said, "How careful do you have to be, carrying this kind of thing?"

"Well, you can't drop it, of course, but the felt does hold the coins pretty well. I can drive over a bumpy road with this in the back of the wagon and not have to worry."

"All right. Anything else?"

"Looseleaf fillers." Billy went over to a shelf and took down a black filler, saying, "Some people keep practically all their stock in books like this. I just do for some high-turnover items, the kind of thing twenty different people might look at before somebody buys."

Parker took the filler and leafed through it. The interior was double-thickness pages of clear plastic, with coins inside against a white paper backing. "These'll be easiest," Parker said.

"Oh, sure. We just pick them up and carry them out. But not many people have these."

"What do most have?"

"The large cases," Billy said promptly. "They'll be partly unpacked into the display cases on all the tables."

"Some of the stuff will still be packed?"

"Oh, sure. Up to, I don't know, maybe a quarter of the coins there. A lot of dealers bring more coins than they can display all at once in the space they're given."

"Good. Anything else?"

Billy looked around, squinting under the fluorescent light. "I guess not. I can't think of anything."

"All right," Parker said. "I have something. Money."

"Money?"

"You're financing this thing," Parker reminded him. "I'm going to need two grand."

"Two thous— What for?"

"Supplies," Parker said.

"But— Two thousand dollars!"

Claire said quietly, "Don't be stupid, Billy."

Billy flushed, his forehead gleaming pink under the light. Not looking at Claire, he said stiffly, "When do you want it?"

"Now."

"The bank's closed by now."

Claire said warningly, "Billy."

Billy licked his lips, frowned, moved his hands vaguely back and forth. "I'll have to— You'll have to look the other way."

Parker shrugged. "Which way's the other way?"

"That way," he said, pointing shakily toward Claire.

Parker and Lempke faced Claire, and listened to Billy getting at a safe at the other end of the room. Claire, leaning against the wall, arms folded, smiled faintly and sardonically at Parker the whole time.

Finally Billy said, "It's okay now."

They turned around and Billy was standing there, embarrassed, holding a white envelope in his hand. Extending it to Parker, he said, "I'm sorry about that. But you can—you can understand how it is."

"Sure." Parker put the envelope in his pocket. "You two go on upstairs," he said. "Lempke and I want to talk."

Lempke raised his head slightly at the sound of his name, then let it sag again. Billy gave him a troubled glance, then smiled nervously and said, "Okay. You want anything to drink?"

"No."

"Or coffee, something like that."

"No."

"Oh. Well—" Billy looked this way and that, returning more and more to his old style. The one thing he couldn't do was make a quick exit.

Claire solved the problem for him this time, saying, "Come along, Billy," and starting up the stairs. Billy gratefully trotted after her, not looking back.

Parker went over and sat on a corner of the mailing table, looking down at Lempke, who was still slumped in his chair, dispiritedly gazing down at the hands curled in his lap. Lempke's hair was thinning; through it his scalp looked gray. His shoulders were as bowed as a coat hanger. Parker said, "All you have to say is, I want out."

Lempke shook his head back and forth, slowly. "I got no place else to go, Parker," he said.

"That's not the question."

Lempke raised his head at last, blinked up at Parker. He looked blind. He said, "What's it gonna need from me?"

"On the caper or before?"

"On. There's nothing before, I know that, nothing I have to sweat about."

"You pack coins," Parker told him.

Lempke rubbed the back of one hand across his mouth. "That's all? No muscle?"

"You're not the man for muscle."

Lempke managed something that looked like a smile. "Don't I know it? I think I could do that."

"So could others," Parker told him. "Guy named Littlefield, maybe you know him."

"For God's sake, Parker," Lempke said, as though he might cry. "I'm the one brought you in on this."

Parker shrugged. He got out his cigarettes, offered one to Lempke. Lempke shook his head. Parker lit a cigarette of his own, tossing the match on the floor. "Sometimes it's tough to know when you should retire," he said. "Some people stick around too long."

"I know when," Lempke said. "After this one, believe me. I got no stake now, it all went to lawyers when I took my fall."

"We could maybe work out a finder's fee. Three per cent, something like that. If the others said okay."

"Finder's fee?" Lempke had the ashen look of a man insulted in a way he can't fathom. "I need to be *in* this," he said.

Parker got up from the table and walked over to one of the display cases and looked inside. The first coin he saw was priced at three hundred fifty dollars. It was just a coin, metal, a little worn.

Lempke said, "From now till it's over, I don't say a word. I don't get cold feet. I don't get in your way."

Looking in at the coins, Parker said, "This train don't carry passengers."

"I'll pull my weight. Whatever happens, I'll pull my weight, I swear it. I never let anybody down my whole life long."

Parker nodded and turned around. "All right," he said. "Let's talk about our string. We'll need two men."

"You've got it doped?"

"Some of it." Parker went back over to the table and sat on its edge again. "We need one with muscle," he said, "to tote things. And one to front the power-company truck."

Lempke frowned, wanting to be helpful. "How about Dan Wycza?" he said. "For the muscle."

"He's dead. What do you hear from Hack Brown?"

"I met him inside. I think he's still there. He killed a woman for some damn reason."

Parker shrugged. Muscle had a habit of being emotional trouble; all right when working, but jumpy as a high-school girl betweentimes.

Lempke said, "I tell you who'd be good. Otto Mainzer."

"Mainzer? Do I know him?"

"He's some sort of crazy Nazi, but he's okay on the job."

"You know how to get in touch with him?"

"In Denver, I think, I'll ask around. What about Jack French, do we bring him back in?"

"He wouldn't come," Parker said.

"Carlow," Lempke said. "Mike Carlow, he'd be perfect."

"I remember Mike," Parker said. "Give him a call." He got to his feet, dropped his cigarette on the cement floor, heeled it out. "I'll be off for a day or two," he said. "Getting the truck."

Lempke said, "What about Billy? He going to be okay?"

"We need him," Parker said.

"I know, but how is he?"

"Claire can keep him on his feet."

"You and Claire are making a thing," Lempke said. "That isn't like you, on the job."

Parker said, "Maybe it's part of the job."

"You mean, you hold Claire and she holds Billy."

"Something like that," Parker said. The truth was different, though, and more complicated. Usually, Parker had no interest in sex while he was working, saving it all for afterwards, but everything had been different this time. He'd gotten interested in Claire before doing any real thinking about the job, and had only started theorizing about the job as a tactic to get Claire. Then the job had turned out to be feasible after all, and Claire was all bound up in it, a part of it. Things would probably change as the night of the heist got closer, but so far his attention was divided in a way not usual with him.

But he wasn't about to explain himself to Lempke, so he just agreed with Lempke's explanation and then they went on upstairs.

They found Billy sitting at the kitchen table, looking sullen. Parker said, "Where is she?"

"In there," Billy said, pointing toward the front room. It was clear he'd tried again to establish his position with Claire, and had gotten the same inevitable putdown.

Parker said, "I want your wagon for a day or two."

Billy shrugged. "I don't care."

Parker turned away from him and went on into the living room, where Claire was sitting as self-absorbed as a cat, doing her nails again. Parker said, "We've got to take a trip for a day or two."

She looked up at him. "All of us?"

"You and me. You'll have to drive the wagon back."

Lempke had come in, and said, "You going to get the truck?"

"Right."

"I'll get in touch with those two boys."

Billy came to the doorway, looking pained. Eyes on Claire, he said, "You're going together?"

Claire gave him an ice-cold look, and said nothing.

Billy started two or three different things to say, failed to say any of them, and abruptly turned around and hurried back to the kitchen.

Parker said to Claire, "Don't push him so hard he falls over."

"Him," she said with contempt, and turned to put the top on the nail polish.

"We need him," Parker said. "Go out to the kitchen and pull the knife out of him."

"He'll be all right."

"Do it anyway."

She turned around, seemed about to tell Parker to go to hell, thought about it, changed her mind, shrugged in sudden irritability, and went out to the kitchen.

Parker said to Lempke, "Tell her I'm in the car."

"See you in a while."

Parker went out and sat behind the wheel. Five minutes later Claire came and slid into the seat beside him. "He'll be good," she said.

Parker looked at her. "And you?"

She sighed and nodded. "I'll be good, too." She handed him the car keys.

3

THEY LEFT Indianapolis Friday morning, heading straight east. They made good time on the stretches of Interstate 70 that were done, bad time on Route 40, finished with a long run across the Pennsylvania Turnpike, and arrived in Baltimore at eight-thirty that night. Parker found a motel in Towson, they unpacked and showered and changed, and then they went downtown for dinner.

Over coffee, Claire said, "I counted sentences."

He'd been thinking about the wall at Diablo Tours. He frowned at her, saying, "What's that?"

"I counted sentences," she said. "How many things you said to me since we got into the car this morning. You know what the score is?"

"What is this?" He was irritated at having his thoughts broken into by some sort of game.

"Twelve," she said. "Twelve times you've spoken to me. That works out to about one sentence every fifty minutes."

He shook his head. "I don't follow you. What's the problem?"

"What did you bring me along for? You don't talk to me, you don't look at me, you don't know I'm here."

"You drive the wagon back," he said.

"Why not take a plane here? Then you don't need me at all."

He shook his head. "The first place we go may not have what I want. The second place is in Trenton. The third place is in Newark. There's more risk than it's worth to rent a car, or steal one, just to drive around the East Coast a day or two."

Bitterly, she said, "We're back to me not mattering."

He put his hands on the table and studied her. "You want me to do a job," he said. "Leave me alone so I can do it."

"All you were doing today was *driving*."

"Do you know how we're going to get into that bourse room?" he asked her. "Do you know how we're going to take the goods out of there? Do you know how we're going to transport the goods away? Do you know how and where we're going to hole up afterwards? Do you know what we're going to do before and during and after to see to it we don't get picked up?"

She seemed startled. "No," she said. "Of course not. I thought you knew all that."

"Some of it," he said. "Some of it I know because I sat down and thought about it. By next Saturday I'll know the rest of it, because I'll have done a lot more thinking about it."

"Oh," she said.

"I was working today. When I'm not working, give me a call, we'll sit around and talk to each other."

"I'm sorry. I didn't think about it that way."

"Now you know," he said, and waved to the waiter for the check.

Back at the motel, he failed to see her look at him questioningly. The wall at Diablo Tours was bothering him. The other side was fine, doubly fine, with the fake French doors and the maroon drapes, but the Diablo Tours side was open and bare and trouble.

There were twin beds. She took the spread off one of them, turned the covers down, fluffed the pillow. He stood near the door, where he'd stopped after coming into the room. His arms were at his sides, his head tilted forward, his eyes focused on the wooden-armed chair across the way and seeing that smooth cream wall of Diablo Tours. She looked at him, hesitated, and went on into the bathroom. When she came back out, wearing a pale blue nightgown, he was still in the same position.

She said, "Aren't you going to get undressed?"

"I'm going to walk," he said, and left the room.

He didn't really want to walk. All he wanted was to be in a place where he could think. He got into the back seat of the station wagon, rested his elbows on his knees, and thought.

An hour later he went back into the room. The light was out

and Claire seemed to be asleep. Parker didn't switch on any lights. In darkness he found the other bed and got into it. After he was settled, Claire made a noise in her throat and rolled over, but that was all.

4

INSIDE THE shack a white plastic portable radio was trying to play the big beat; it sounded like a grasshopper fight. Hubcaps were mounted all over the walls. On the desk were papers and wrenches. A thin layer of black automobile grease seemed to be smeared over everything, including the kid sitting at the teletype machine, reading the incoming dealer requests.

The kid hadn't looked around when Parker stepped in. Parker waited five seconds, then went over and switched off the radio. The kid snapped around, ready to fight the world, righteous and ugly. He was probably nineteen and a half. He shouted, over the silence, "Whatcha think you're doin'?"

"I want to see Buster."

"You leave that goddam radio alone," the kid said. He got to his feet and came hustling over toward it.

Parker said, "Don't do it."

The kid couldn't believe it. He filled out his black T-shirt just like the pictures in the muscle ads; nobody should kick sand in *his* face. But he was surprised enough to look at Parker before doing anything, and what he saw didn't reassure him. Leaving the radio off, he said, "Buster ain't here. He went surfin'."

"I called this morning, kid, he expects me. Go get him."

"You talked to Buster?"

"Get him."

The kid looked at the radio, at Parker, out the doorway at the wagon sitting there in the sunlight. Claire was in there on the passenger side. She had the windows rolled up because of Buster's Dobermans, even though Parker had told her they wouldn't attack unless ordered. Both dogs were pacing back and forth around the wagon, heads down, nervous and waiting.

The kid shrugged and said, "I can't leave here. I got to watch things in here. Buster'll be back in a little while."

"One," Parker said. "Two."

The kid didn't know what number was the top. He went out the door before Parker could say three.

Parker went over to the teletype and looked at what was coming in. A dealer in Virginia wanted a left front door for a '61 Pontiac Bonneville convertible. As Parker watched, he got one from Wilmington, Delaware.

The door opened and Buster came in, grinning, saying, "Artie tells me you're a redneck bastard."

"How are you, Buster?"

"Just lovely. That your woman out there?"

"Yes," Parker said, because it was easiest to say that.

"Good gash," Buster said, and went over to the teletype for a quick look. He was a big man, with a weight-lifter's body, all shoulder and chest, narrow in the waist. His trousers were stiff with grease, and the sport shirt he wore was no particular color. His hair was pale blond, crewcut, and beneath the grime on his face and arms could be seen a deep tan. He shook his head at the teletype and said, "Nobody wants Plymouth parts. I'm up to the ass in Plymouth parts." Turning away, he said, "Used to be Ford, now it's Plymouth. You wouldn't be after Plymouth parts, would you?"

Parker took out an envelope from his jacket pocket and handed it over. Inside were the color Polaroid shots Lempke had taken of the electric company worktruck.

Buster looked at the photos and began to smile. "You're up to something," he said. He grinned at Parker. "Who you got driving?"

"Maybe Mike Carlow."

"He's okay," Buster said grudgingly. "Not as good as I was." When Parker didn't say anything to that, Buster said, "Am I right, or am I right?"

Buster had bought this yard out of proceeds from half a dozen jobs he'd driven for. He'd been a conscientious driver, imaginative, unshakable in the clutch, but maybe a little too cowboy sometimes. Parker said, "You want to drive for us?"

"Little Buster?" He laughed and shook his head. "I'm where I like to be, pal."

"What can you do me on the truck?"

"International Harvester. Cab's no problem. Have to dummy up something in back. When do you need it?"

"Now."

Buster grinned. "It's always now." He sat down at the desk, studied the photos some more. "Phone company," he said. "Any gas and electric company. Some television repair guys. Maybe— Hold on a second."

Parker waited while Buster made two phone calls. After the second, Buster said, "Screwed-up fender. Let's see what we can do." He went over to the teletype.

When Buster was done typing, Parker said, "You can do it?"

"Sure. Perfect match."

"Paint job?"

Buster shook his head. "That's not me. You get that done someplace else."

"Where?"

"You don't know anybody around here?"

"This is your town, not mine."

Buster scratched his nose. "I don't like to be connected," he said. "You know how it is."

"I can't hit somebody cold. I need you to clear me."

"Yeah, I know." Buster lit a cigarette, made a face like it tasted bad, and said, "Okay. I'll call the guy. But you make delivery."

"Sure."

"You're going to have no papers on this beast," Buster said. "She's a scrapped truck, she don't exist anymore."

"Naturally."

"Okay. You want anything special under the hood?"

"No."

"The one I got, we'll have to put a new engine in anyway. A different engine, I mean. It can be whatever you want."

"I don't figure to race any cops out of town."

"Whatever you say," Buster pulled a memo pad close. "About money," he said.

"Do it in round numbers."

"The roundest," Buster said. "One G."

"Delivery when?"

"Tonight. Two o'clock. It'll be outside the gate, across the road there, by them trees. Key under the seat."

"Good." Parker took out another envelope, peeled ten hundreds of Billy's money off the stack, dropped it on the desk. He said, "Where's the painter?"

"Lemme check with him first."

Parker waited through another phone call, and then Buster said, "Okay, it's fine. You bring it straight there. He'll want a C and a half."

"That's a hell of a lot for a paint job."

Buster shrugged. "You know how it is," he said. "It's the lettering on the doors. And the risk. And the silence. You want to argue with him, fine by me."

"He's pushing the price a little."

"You're probably right. But he's the only guy I know that I'd trust."

"Then it's good. Where do I find him?"

"He's out by the airport. Take the Harbor Tunnel. You know Baltimore?"

"Not that good."

Buster opened a desk drawer, took out a greasy city map, opened it onto his desk, and showed Parker how to get from there to the paint shop. As he was finishing up, the kid came in, carrying a rusty bumper guard. Pointedly ignoring Parker, he said to Buster, "This is the best I could find."

"You can throw that in the bay," Buster told him. "I told you clean."

"This is the best I could find."

Buster shrugged. Then, grinning, he said, "How come I come in here and the radio's off? Don't you like that music no more?"

Parker didn't like pointless needling. While the kid was trying to find an answer, Parker went over and turned the radio on. Buster looked at him in amused surprise, and the kid just looked baffled.

Outside, the Dobermans watched Parker get into the car, waiting for somebody to tell them to stop him.

The car was full of smoke. Parker rolled a window down and started the engine and drove out of the yard.

Claire said, "Any luck?"

Parker looked at her. "You want to know, or you making small talk?"

"I'm in this, too," she said. "You don't have to push me out all the time."

"We've got a truck," he said. "We come back tonight and take it to where they paint it."

"How are you going to take it back to Indianapolis? Won't it look funny, an Indianapolis Power and Light Company truck on the Pennsylvania Turnpike?"

"We dummy it up with a tarp," he said, and all at once he saw how to do the Diablo Tours wall.

She looked at him and said, "What's the matter?"

"Matter? Why?"

"You're smiling," she said.

He put his hand on her knee. "Because things are good," he said.

He drove one-handed a while, his other hand still resting on her knee.

Claire said, "Where are we going now?"

"Back to the room."

5

AT NIGHT the yard was floodlit, looking like some metallic moonscape where nothing had ever lived. The truck was in total darkness under the trees on the other side of the road.

When Parker stopped the wagon, lights off, near the truck, the two Dobermans came loping out of the yard wreckage to the fence. They did no barking, made no sound at all, but just kept moving restlessly back and forth the other side of the fence, trying to find a way through.

"Those dogs," Claire said, shivering.

Parker touched her shoulder. "They're all right. They mind their business, we mind ours."

"All right." She smiled nervously and squeezed his hand. "Let's hurry out of here."

"Right."

Parker got out of the car and walked over to the truck. When he opened the door no interior light went on. He fumbled around on the dash, found the light switch, pulled it halfway on, and used the dashlight to help him look for the key. Once he got it, he slid behind the wheel and started the engine. The clutch seemed loose to him, and he was already anticipating bad brakes, but it didn't matter. The truck had to be a prop for a while, and then it had to carry the goods away, that's all anybody expected from it. That, and to get back to Indianapolis in the first place.

Claire had already made her U-turn, her headlights flashing over the restless pacing dogs behind the fence, so Parker shifted into first and started along the dirt road, the truck taking the bumps much harder than the wagon had. In the mirror mounted outside the door Parker could see the wagon's lights jouncing along in his wake.

They went out to Philadelphia Road and headed south. Twenty-five minutes later, Parker took the Airport exit from the Baltimore-Washington Expressway, turned off onto Fort Meade Road, and then went on more slowly, having trouble seeing street signs in the dark. Claire did better than Parker had expected, staying a good distance back, making them less of a caravan.

It was quarter to three when he finally stopped the truck in front of a squat white concrete block building bearing the many-colored sign PALETTE AUTO PAINTING. An overhead garage door in the building front immediately opened, and a short round man in a black suit came out, cigar in the middle of his face, waving his arms frantically for Parker to drive on inside. Parker did, and the round man slid the door down again and came trotting over to say, "They's a station wagon out there."

"It's with me," Parker said. He shut off the engine and climbed out of the cab.

"Well, they ought to turn off their lights," the round man said.

"Go tell her yourself." Parker took out the envelope of pictures, saying, "This is what I want it to look like."

"Not me," said the round man, waving his hands back and forth. "Not me, I'm not the man for that." Raising his voice, he shouted past Parker, "Hey, Wemm!"

Parker turned and saw coming toward him a Negro in green coveralls. He had the self-contained movements of a man about to be asked to show how good he is, a man who knows he's more than good enough. His hair was gray, but he had the face of a young man.

"Show your stuff to Wemm," the round man said. "He's the one knows all about this."

"What do you do?" Parker asked.

"I'm the boss," the round man said. "Is she gonna leave those lights on out there?"

"I don't know." Parker turned his back on the round man and said to Wemm, "You want to see these pictures?"

"They might help," Wemm said.

Parker handed them over, Wemm skimmed through them briefly, and then shook his head. "Come along," he said, and started away.

The room they were in was large and open, with a cement floor. Pipes and hoses crisscrossed on the ceiling. Fluorescent lights made the place as bright as day. Over on the right, three late-model automobiles were masked and taped, waiting for the spray.

Wemm led Parker to a small glass-windowed cubicle on the left. Inside were a cluttered desk and two chairs. Wemm motioned to Parker to take one chair, while he took the one at the desk. He spread the photographs out on the clutter atop the desk and bent the fluorescent desk lamp closer to them. After squinting at the pictures a minute, he said to Parker, "How's this color reproduction? Any good?"

"How do I know?"

"You might look. Is this the same color as the real truck or isn't it?"

Parker leaned over and studied the nearest photo, then said, "I think it's brighter. Not much."

Wemm nodded. "I thought so," he said. "It's what you might call institutional orange. All the same people that put that puke green in all the hallways, when it comes time to paint a truck, this is the color they use."

"You know the color, then."

"It ain't gonna be easy to match."

"Why not? If you already know it—"

"This is a private place. What we do is cars, private passenger cars." He tapped one of the photos. "This isn't what you could call a popular color for private passenger cars."

Parker sat back. "Can't you do it?"

"Sure I can do it."

"Then what's all the talk?"

Wemm spread his hands. "I want you to understand the problems we got to face here."

"Why?"

"What's that?"

"Why do I have to understand the problems you got to face

here?"

"Well—" Wemm blinked, and looked at the photos, and shook his head. "Be damned if I know," he said. He gave Parker a small wondering smile. "Just shooting off my mouth, I guess."

Parker said, "When will it be done?"

"You want to take it out tomorrow night, don't you?"

"If I can."

"You can."

"I'll need it covered with a tarp or something."

Wemm nodded. "The body. That's no problem. And over the name on the doors, we put a piece of cardboard with masking tape, put some other company name on it. You got any favorites?"

"No."

"Then that's it. I'll need to keep the pictures."

"Naturally." Parker got to his feet. "I'll want it delivered."

"You talk to the boss about that," Wemm said. "That, and money."

"All right."

Parker found the boss out by the overhead door. "I'll want it delivered tomorrow night," he said.

"Delivered? What's the matter with your chauffeur out there?"

"She won't be here."

"Delivered." He took the cigar out of his mouth, shook his head. "That's extra."

"Five," Parker said.

"I don't know—"

"Don't push so hard," Parker told him. "You'll get another customer some day."

The round man shrugged with sudden irritation and said, "The hell with it. It's all in the same price. Don't worry about it."

"Good." Parker handed over a hundred and fifty of Billy's dollars, and the round man said, "You want a receipt?"

"No," Parker said.

"Of course not," said the round man. "That was a dumb question, you know that?"

"Yes," Parker said.

He gave the round man the name of the motel in Towson, and then went out to the car. Claire had already moved over, and when Parker slid in she said, "How'd it go?"

"Good. They"ll deliver it tomorrow night."

"You don't want me to drive you down?"

"You can go back now, everything's set. And I'll take longer in the truck than you in this."

She said, "You want me to go back now?"

"Why not?"

"Tonight, you mean?"

He looked at her, and finally understood what she was driving at. His mood of exhilaration from this afternoon had worn off by now, he was back to concentrating on the job, but she had no way to know that.

There were times when you had to push yourself a little to keep somebody else in the string content, and this was one of the times. In a way Lempke had been right, after all; Claire was valuable, if only to keep Billy in line.

Parker squeezed her knee. "Not tonight," he said. "Tomorrow morning's soon enough, isn't it?"

The look she gave him was knowing. "Tomorrow morning's fine," she said, a touch of irony in her voice.

6

THE TRUCK was delivered at one-thirty in the morning, driven by a skinny young kid in T-shirt and glasses. He was full of repressed excitement, a kid in the middle of a game of cops and robbers.

What Parker could see of the paint job looked good, but he couldn't see much. The entire body was covered with a dirty gray tarp, tied down along the sides. The pieces of cardboard on the doors said, in black letters on white, THE WEMM CORPORATION.

Parker looked the truck over by the light from the motel sign, and told the kid, "It's okay."

"Mister Reejus said you'd give me cabfare."

"He did, huh." Parker gave the kid a five, and the kid took off at a half-trot, looking over his shoulder, on his way fast to tell somebody about his adventure. Parker just hoped he'd been brought in after the truck was already masked.

His bag was packed, the room all paid for. He preferred to do as much of his driving as possible at night, since the plates on the truck were probably no good, and in any case he had no papers for it. They were D.C. plates; he could replace them with Indiana plates the day of the job.

Parker took Interstate 83 up to Harrisburg, then headed west on the Pennsylvania Turnpike. The truck was a little better than he'd expected. Above fifty-five it had a bad front-end shimmy, but right on fifty-five it seemed ready to roll forever. He made good time, all things considered, and didn't mind the cars that streamed by him on his left.

It was just noon when he arrived in Indianapolis. Because it was Sunday, he got involved in church-leaving traffic, and it took him forty-five minutes to get across town and into Mars Hill. The station wagon was gone from Billy's driveway, so Parker drove on in, turned around the back of the house, and left the truck in the backyard, near the barbecue.

Billy came out the kitchen door as Parker came walking away from the truck, carrying his suitcase. Billy said, "That's gonna leave marks in the lawn. Tire marks."

"You want to leave it out front? Raise questions?"

Billy looked pained. He gazed at the new tire marks in the grass and shook his head. "If it has to be—"

"It has to be," Parker said, and went on by him and into the house.

Billy followed him in, saying, "Lempke had to go away. To see somebody named Mainzer. He said he'd be back Tuesday. And we're supposed to meet a man named Mike Carlow at the airport tomorrow afternoon at three-thirty."

"Where's Claire?"

Billy's face clouded. "Home, I guess," he said, suddenly sullen.

"Call her. Tell her to come pick me up."

"She doesn't like me to wake her."

"She won't mind this time," Parker said. He opened the refrigerator and took out a bottle of beer. "Where's the opener?"

"On the wall there. See it?"

Parker uncapped the beer and went on into the living room. He sat on a chair arm and watched nothing happening out on the street. From the kitchen he could hear Billy's whining voice as he spoke on the telephone.

A few minutes later Billy came in and said, "She says she'll be here in half an hour."

Parker nodded.

Billy stood in the middle of the room, shifting his weight back and forth, fiddling with his fingers. Parker kept looking out of the window. A little girl in a pink dress went by on a red tricycle. A black Buick convertible, its radio playing rock and roll, cruised by with its top down. The two kids inside it wore their hair as long as Veronica Lake.

Billy said, "About Claire."

Parker uptilted the beer bottle, swallowed, looked out at the street.

Billy cleared his throat. He said, "You don't want her. I mean, not really. Not to marry or anything like that."

Parker turned his head and looked at Billy and said, "You can't let it alone, can you?"

"You may not believe this," Billy said earnestly, "but I love that girl. I really do. I'm in love with her."

Parker looked out the window again.

"I mean," Billy said, "when this is all over, you'll just go away and leave her here. Right? It doesn't mean anything to you, it's just a girl for now, for a few days, while you're here."

Parker nodded. "That's what you want to hear," he said. "That the competition's going away."

"Well. This sort of thing happens to you all the time, doesn't it? I mean, you meet a girl, it's just for a little while, then you move on, you go someplace else, it's all over."

Parker watched the street. What Billy had just said was right, had become increasingly right in the last few years. As women had become less individually important to him, a faceless quantity of them had become much more important. As though he were in some strange way really monogamous, true to a faceless nameless personality-less body, so that he never involved himself with anyone else, only her, time after time after time.

He had been married once, but she was dead now. She'd gotten into a bind, where she'd had the choice of risking her own life or betraying Parker, and she'd chosen betrayal. When Parker had come looking for her afterwards, unsure in his own mind what he meant to do about it, she'd killed herself. Out of panic, probably, rather than remorse. But since her, since Lynn, there had been no woman, not for long. Never long enough for him and the woman to become individuals to one another.

Looking at it now, he could see where it had served as an answer to the problem of Lynn's betrayal, but it was the kind of answer which—like drugs—required larger and larger application, led eventually to sloppiness and excess, became eventually as bad a problem as the one it was supposed to be solving.

Because Claire had come into his life in an odd way, entering in conjunction with a job, almost becoming part of the work at hand, she'd managed somehow to break through that pattern he'd developed. He found himself wanting to please her, willing to go out of his way for her sake, and though he'd been giving himself practical reasons to explain it—she could handle Billy, and so on—the truth was he acted that way because he wanted to.

What about when it was over, when the job was done? For the first time in several years, he didn't know what would happen then. He might flee from Claire as he had fled from all the others. Or he might want her to stay with him for a while; a year, a month. Or he might want her to stay with him permanently. Right now he had no way to tell which it was going to be.

But he knew which one Billy wanted to hear, and the easiest way to keep Billy happy was to tell him what he wanted to hear. Still looking out at the street, Parker said, "When the caper's over, I leave. By myself."

"That's what I figured," Billy said, and Parker could hear the happy smile in his voice. Then Billy started walking around in the living room, behind Parker, and after a minute he said, "You know, Claire and me, we don't—"

"Don't start," Parker said. He turned around and looked at Billy. "I don't want your reminiscences."

"Oh," Billy said, and suddenly looked frightened, as though it had just occurred to him that it was possible for him to make some wrong move, say some wrong word, and Parker would change his mind and stay. He looked around the room, licked his lips, made vague arm movements, and at last said, "Well, I guess I better—" And hurried away to the kitchen.

Parker shook his head. He continued to drink his beer and look out the window, thinking about nothing at all, until the station wagon pulled into the driveway. Then he got his suitcase and went outside.

Claire had moved over, but Parker opened the passenger door and said, "You drive."

"Okay," she said, and slid back. When Parker was in and the

door shut, she said, "Back to the hotel?"

"No. I checked out of there. We shouldn't be seen around there anymore, none of us."

"Where, then? Some other hotel?"

"Not good."

She looked at him. "My place?"

"Your place," he said.

7

THE MEETING was in Claire's apartment, ten o'clock Tuesday evening. Claire and Parker were already there, and Billy arrived early, at nine-forty-five. Lempke and Mike Carlow showed up at ten on the dot, and Otto Mainzer came along five minutes later.

The apartment was on the third floor of a new building, all glass and chrome outside, all plasterboard and corner-cutting inside. There was a long living room with windows at one end overlooking an interior court, a small square bedroom with a narrow window overlooking an airshaft, and a midget kitchen and bathroom, windowless, sharing an air duct.

The furnishings showed a combination of taste and haste, the creation of a woman who wants good surroundings but doesn't intend to stay in this particular location very long. Sofa, lamps, tables, drapes, all had discreet elegance and were quietly but obviously expensive, but there were gaps, empty spaces, almost as though someone had come through and removed every fourth item from the room. There were no paintings on the walls, for instance, and no lamp handy to the armchair near the window, and no table on the right side of the sofa.

Before the meeting, Claire had said to Parker, "This may sound silly, but should there be any refreshments or anything? I mean, should I get some beer or anything like that?"

"Be a good idea to have some stuff on hand," Parker said. "But don't do any bridge club number, bringing in the little sandwiches on the tray."

"I know better than that," she said.

When Billy arrived, Claire was still getting dressed. Parker opened the door and Billy came in saying, "I guess I'm early."

"Go sit down," Parker told him, and shut the door.

Billy was at his most nervous, looking around like a possum coming out of a hole. He settled in a chair at the far end of the living room, and sat there fidgeting.

Parker couldn't stand to be around such restlessness, so he went into the bedroom and sprawled on the bed there and watched Claire dress.

She was a good woman, good to look at and good to be with. Sensible and independent. Not full of foolishness.

Looking at her now, as she moved around the room in bra and panties, he felt no immediate desire for her, but that was because he was thinking mostly about the work, the meeting, the personalities. Still, there was a background aura of remembered pleasure, and the good feeling of watching a body he had known. There would be time to bring the memories up to date, afterward.

By the time the bell rang she was ready, wearing pale green stretch pants and a green and pink and white blouse. "I'll get it this time," she said, and they went out of the bedroom together.

The look Billy gave them was full of pain, seeing them emerging together from the bedroom, but they both ignored him. Parker went to the kitchen and opened himself a beer, and when he came back to the living room Lempke was there with Mike Carlow.

Carlow was a narrow rawboned guy, a little shorter than medium height. He was about forty, with the leathery face and washed-out eyes of a man who spends most of his time outdoors. His nose was long and narrow, lips thin, Adam's apple prominent. He said, "Hello, Parker. Long time no see."

"There's beer," Parker told him.

"Good. Want one, Lempke?"

"Not for me, thanks," said Lempke. He smiled apologetically and patted his stomach. "Belly's acting up," he said.

Carlow went on into the kitchen, and Parker said to Lempke, "How much does he know?"

"Most of it. That he's supposed to drive, that it's a break-in with armed guards, that it's valuable coins and we've got a dealer to fence. And that there's five of us in it, with shares to be worked out."

"All right. You introduce him to Billy."

"Sure."

Lempke went away, and Claire came over to say, "Should I leave when the meeting starts?"

"No. You're in it."

She looked surprised. "I am?"

"It's your caper, remember? You started it going."

"So I'm going to be a part of it."

"That's right."

She shrugged. "If you don't mind amateurs," she said.

"You'll do your part all right."

"Thank you." The bell sounded, and she said, "I'll get it."

Lempke and Carlow and Billy were all standing at the far end of the room now, talking together. Billy was looking eager, Lempke sick, Carlow indrawn and waiting. Parker waited by the kitchen door, watching Claire in the short hall, opening the front door.

It was Otto Mainzer, a burly tall man dressed in black. His hair was so pale blond, and cut so short, that in most lights he looked bald. His face was dominated by a large hook nose with flaring nostrils. Eyes and mouth were both thin, flat, pale. The expression he seemed habitually to be trying for was arrogance, but instead he looked merely irritated. When he saw Claire a surprised smile creased his face, looking strange there, as though it had been delivered to the wrong address. He said something to Claire, Parker didn't hear what, but he saw her stiffen. Her reply was short and curt, and Mainzer's smile turned cynical. "Sure thing," he said, and came on into the apartment.

Parker went over to him and shook his hand, saying, "Good to see you."

"Been a few years," Mainzer said. He looked as though he should be speaking with an accent, but he was native-born and the only trace in his speech was a touch of Boston.

"We're all here," Parker said. "Come on over. Lempke tell you the situation?"

"Coins. We got a tame dealer."

"Right."

Mainzer nodded his head at Claire. "Lempke didn't say anything about that."

"Why should he?"

Mainzer looked at him in surprise, and then laughed. "Still the same," he said. "The same bloodless bastard you always were. What about her? She belong to anybody?"

"Me."

"Come off it, Parker."

Parker shrugged, and walked off toward the other end of the room. After a second Mainzer followed. Claire had already joined the group at the other end.

Mainzer and Carlow knew each other, and Lempke made the necessary introductions to Billy and Claire. Then they all sat down, here and there around the living room, and Parker told them the setup.

When he was done, Mainzer said, "What's the shares?"

Parker said, "Lebatard takes fifty per cent. The second fifty. We get ours out of the first stuff he sells."

"What happens to our half?"

"We split it four ways. You, Carlow, Lempke, me."

"What about the little lady here?"

"She gets hers out of Lebatard's half."

Claire looked faintly amused at that, and Billy looked—for just a second—beside himself with pleasure.

Mainzer glanced at Claire, then at Billy, then back at Parker. He grinned and shook his head. "Nothing stays simple," he said. "Not even my old buddy Parker."

Carlow said, "What do we do afterward?"

"Hole up at Lebatard's. In the cellar for a day or two."

Billy said, "Why in the cellar? I have room upstairs, you can—"

Parker said to him, "If I was a cop, and a coin convention was knocked over, I might come around to a local coin dealer for a little chat."

Billy looked startled. "You think they will?"

Lempke said, "Billy, didn't you already figure that?"

"Why should they come to me?"

Lempke said, "For background information, number one. And just in case you were in on it, number two."

Parker said, "You better think about it some, start getting used to the idea. So you don't start signing confessions the minute they walk through the door."

Billy chewed his lower lip. He gave Claire a look of helplessness and fright, but she was facing the other way.

Carlow said, "One problem."

Parker looked at him. "What's that?"

"This looks like a job we can't case ahead of time."

"We look it over Friday night," Parker said. "The Pinkerton people should use the same setup both nights."

"Doesn't give us much time."

"It should be enough," Parker said. "You want in?"

Carlow drank beer, stalling a bit, and then said, "What I do, I bring the truck in place, I set it up, I front for it. You people bring the boodle down, we stow it, I drive away. There shouldn't be any law on my tail, right?"

"Right."

"I mean, I don't outrace anybody."

"Not with the truck I got us, no."

Carlow nodded. "Good. I see law, I leave the truck and light a shuck on my feet."

"Naturally."

"Then I'm in," Carlow said.

"Good." Parker turned to Mainzer. "What about you, Otto?"

"I'm the mule," Mainzer said. "I carry a ton of coins downstairs."

"Right."

Mainzer flexed an arm and looked at it. "I always get the brainwork," he said.

"I've got brainwork for you," Parker told him.

"What's that?"

"You in?"

"Sure I'm in. I come here, didn't I? I listened, didn't I? I stayed here, didn't I? What's the brainwork?"

Parker said, "We've got to go through the Diablo Tours wall tomorrow night."

Lempke said, "Why so early?"

"By Thursday they'll be setting up for the convention.

Tomorrow night's the last time we get the ballroom to ourselves."

Lempke said, "But what about the woman at Diablo Tours? She'll see the hole."

"That was the hang-up," said Parker. "But then I remembered about Otto here. He's got a specialty."

Lempke said, "You want to burn the building down?"

Parker turned to Mainzer. "I want a fire in their office. Tonight. It ought to do enough damage so they have to close shop for a few days. It ought to do a lot of damage to the inner office and especially around the rear wall. But it shouldn't be arson."

Mainzer grinned. "Short circuit," he said. "Faulty wiring. Easiest thing in the world. But that's extra, Parker."

Parker held on for a second, not wanting to say anything to drive Mainzer away, because regardless of his personality he was a good addition to the string. Then he said, "We'll all be doing extras, Otto. It'll even out."

Mainzer scratched his bald-looking head. "I don't know, Parker," he said. "That sort of thing, fires and all, that's mostly private with me. I mean, you want me in the string for strong-arm, right? A mule, that's my specialty. Now, this other stuff—"

Parker said, "You don't have to stick around, Otto."

Mainzer looked surprised, then grinned again and shook his head. "It's late in the season to replace me," he said.

"Then I'll have to get on the phone right now," Parker said, and got to his feet.

Mainzer frowned, sitting forward. "You wouldn't really do that," he said.

Parker stood by his chair, half-turned away, looking back and down at Mainzer. He was running a bluff, and they both knew it, but he was prepared to have the bluff called and to start looking for a replacement right now, and they both had to know that, too. It was a bluff with teeth in it. He said, "Make up your mind, Otto. Are you in or out?"

Mainzer studied Parker's face, and began to crack his knuckles one by one, starting with the thumb on his left hand and continuing all the way through to the little finger on his right. When he was all done he grinned, and shrugged, and looked around at the rest of them, saying, "What the hell. It's a donation. For the cause."

Parker said, "Good." Still standing, he turned and said, "What about you, Lempke? Still in?"

Lempke looked surprised, then apprehensive, then determined. "Still in," he said.

"All right. Otto sets the fire tonight. Tomorrow night, Otto, Mike, Lempke and I go in and make the hole. Claire, you go to the hotel tomorrow afternoon, take a room for one night on a low floor, the lowest you can get. Lempke and Mike case the layout Friday night. Billy, you check out all the dealers Friday, be ready to give us a map Friday night showing the locations of the tables we want to hit."

"Oh, sure," said Billy. "I can do that."

"We meet here tomorrow night at two, all except Billy." Parker looked around. "Anything else?"

There was nothing else, and they all relaxed. Carlow went to the kitchen for more beer, and Mainzer told a dirty joke, telling it to the group but mostly to Claire, who ignored him. Lempke and Carlow got into reminiscences about mutual friends.

Lempke and Carlow were the first to leave, followed shortly by Mainzer, who had given up on Claire and was now pretending she didn't exist. Billy hung around a while longer, until Claire told him she was tired and going to bed and he had to leave. He went reluctantly, but quietly.

When they were alone, Claire said to Parker, "That man Carlow seems all right. Very professional and competent."

"He knows his business."

"I don't know about the other one," she said.

"I do," Parker said. "Otto knows his business, too. He'll do what he's here for."

"What about Billy?" she said. "Are you sure it's safe to stay at his place afterwards? What if the police come and he loses his nerve?"

"He'll keep his nerve better knowing I'm a wall away."

"If you say so," she said, and shrugged, and changed the subject.

Much later, in bed, they heard a distant wail of sirens. Claire shifted position in the dark and whispered, "Is that Mister Mainzer's fire?"

"I don't know. I suppose so."

Parker lay on his back and listened to the sound, and then to the following silence. For the thousandth time, he found himself wishing the other members of a string could leave their personalities at home when they came to a job, but of course practically nobody ever could. Otto would do his work well, and had undoubtedly done the fire well, but between now and Saturday night Otto could be guaranteed to rub everybody else the wrong way at least once each. But the only thing to do was try to ignore him, concentrate instead on the job.

Claire moved again, and put one arm across his chest. He shifted closer to her, and shut his eyes, and after a while stopped listening to the post-siren silence and went to sleep.

8

IT HAD been a good fire, just exactly right. The outer office of Diablo Tours was smoke-streaked and waterlogged, the inner office was badly charred and burnt. The desk in there was a blackened shell, and the rear wall had been badly damaged by the fire. No one would be working here for a while, not until the place was redone, which wouldn't start happening until after the insurance adjusters and fire department investigators were through, which was unlikely to take less than a week.

Parker and Carlow and Mainzer arrived a little after two in the morning. The door had been locked and a piece of plywood nailed over the hole in it where the firemen had knocked out the frosted glass panel, but the lock was an easy one and they went through it practically without stopping. Parker had previously worked out the best route in here, trying it by day, going through the hotel, up to the roof and through a corridor window into this building, which was several stories taller than the hotel. From there it was simple to come down the stairs and through the locked door into the wreckage of Diablo Tours, which smelled inside of dampness and charred wood.

When they entered the inner office, Mainzer looked around and smiled in satisfaction, saying, "Nice job. Admit it, Parker, it's a nice job."

"You did fine," Parker said, both because it was true and because there was the necessity to keep Mainzer happy. There was always the necessity to keep people happy, that was why Parker seldom got along with people away from work. When a job was at stake he was willing to make the effort, but otherwise he wasn't.

They couldn't use any light of their own in here, not even a flashlight, but the same streetlight that illuminated the ballroom in the hotel next door also shone in the window here, its bluish-white light softening the effects of the fire, making the room like a small stage setting before a performance.

The wall was plasterboard, and the fire had exposed some of the lines of separation between the panels. Parker went to the corner of the wall farthest from the window and felt along the edge of the panel there. "This will do," he said.

Carlow had brought along a small toolkit, which he now put on the desk. They got screwdrivers and pliers from it and went to work on the plasterboard panel, removing all the nails holding it to the supports, not worrying about gouging the wall. While Carlow worked on the left side and Parker on the right, Mainzer removed the molding from the bottom of the panel and then stood on a chair to remove a narrow strip of wood where the wall met the ceiling.

It took fifteen minutes to completely free the panel, which was four feet wide and ran from floor to ceiling. When they were done, they leaned the panel forward slightly and slid it to one side, then rested it back against the wall beside the new hole.

Inside, there were two-by-fours in a vertical-horizontal network, plus electric cables, and backed by a wall of concrete block. While Mainzer went to work with a small saw, removing some of the two-by-fours, Parker and Carlow began chipping away at the cement between the concrete blocks.

This part took longer, but by three-thirty they had pulled out eleven blocks, leaving a hole five feet high and about two feet wide, unobstructed by either two-by-fours or electric cables. On the other side of the hole was a blank sheet of plywood.

It was cumbersome to get at the plywood, but they managed at last to drill a series of holes in it and then to get to work on it with the saw, and in half an hour they had the plywood taken out in four pieces and were looking at a blank gray French door.

This was one of the doors Parker had seen in the ballroom, behind the maroon plush curtain. Apparently, in the days before this building had been here, there had been some sort of balcony or terrace off the hotel's ballroom, to which the French doors had led. When this building was erected the French doors were nailed shut on the inside, covered with sheets of plywood on the outside, and more or less forgotten.

Parker reached in with a screwdriver handle and tapped the door twice. Lempke was supposed to be on the other side, was to have been in the ballroom since three o'clock—over an hour now—to let them know when it was safe to make the final breakthrough.

Parker's knock was almost immediately followed by three slow raps from the other side. That meant everything was safe. If other people had been around, or if for any reason Lempke had wanted them to wait, his answer would have been two fast taps.

Mainzer did most of the last part. The door had been nailed into its frame, and Mainzer now had to pry it loose, while standing crouched half in and half out of a hole five feet high with jagged edges of plywood all around its perimeter. Nails came out slowly, reluctantly, with shrill squeals, as Mainzer forced the door away from its frame an inch at a time. Mainzer had to stop and rest twice, but after the second time the door suddenly gave all at once, fell away from the frame, and leaned sagging against the maroon curtain on the other side.

Mainzer stepped back, grinning, pleased with himself; beads of perspiration on his forehead gleamed like quicksilver in the dim blue-white light. He made an after-you gesture at the hole, saying, "There you go, Parker."

Carlow said, "We did a little bit, too, Otto."

Mainzer turned to make a sharp answer, but Parker said, "Let's see what it looks like on the other side." He stepped between them, diverting them, and led the way through the hole, wrestling the door off to one side.

The nearest break in the drapes was a few feet to the right, being held open by Lempke, who was just a dim small silhouette in the darkness. As Parker came through, Lempke whispered, "Christ, you made noise in there. I been hearing you half an hour."

"Anybody come by?"

"No, but they could've."

Parker stepped out of the way, and Carlow came through, carrying a pair of pliers and a screwdriver. He said, "I left the kit on the desk in there."

"Good." Parker stepped closer to Carlow and said, under his breath, "Let Otto run on. It doesn't hurt anything."

Carlow shrugged in irritation. "If you say so."

"It's best. See you up in the room."

"Right."

Parker went back through the hole to the travel office, where Mainzer was waiting, leaning against a wall with his arms folded. Parker said, "It's okay."

"Fine." Mainzer came off the wall and flexed his shoulders. "What's the matter with Carlow? Got the wind up?"

"Let him talk," Parker said. "It doesn't hurt anything."

"Sure. What do I care?"

The two of them went to work, putting the concrete blocks back where they were, filling the interior of the hole again. The sawed-off sections of two-by-four and the pieces of plywood were stacked up in front of the concrete blocks, and then the plasterboard panel was put back in place and the nails pushed back into the original nail holes. When they were done the wall looked almost the same as before, but could be gone through in a minimum of time.

Parker picked up the toolkit, checked to be sure they had everything, and then he and Mainzer left, going back the way they'd come, up and over the hotel roof and down the stairs inside the hotel to the room Claire had taken that afternoon.

Carlow and Lempke were already there, having rigged up the door again on the ballroom side. Lempke said, "You chipped a lot of paint off, around the edges of the door. It doesn't look the same as the rest anymore."

"Nobody will see it," Parker told him.

Carlow said, "That's what I said before."

Parker said to Lempke, "You go first. See you at Lebatard's place Saturday night."

"Right. Right."

Lempke went out, and Parker went over to the closet, got out the empty overnight bag Claire had checked in with, and put the toolkit inside it.

Mainzer said, "This thing has the smell, Parker. The sweet smell. I always know."

"That's good," Parker said.

Carlow had looked at Mainzer in disgust, but hadn't said anything. Now he got to his feet and said, "I'll go now. See you Saturday, Parker."

"Right."

After Carlow had left, Mainzer said, "What is he, Parker, do you know?"

"What do you mean, what is he?"

"What kine of name is Carlow? Is it Jewish?"

Parker looked at him and didn't say anything.

Mainzer spread his hands. "Don't get me wrong," he said, "I'll work with anybody. Just so they know their job, that's all."

"That's the way to be," Parker said.

"I was just wondering, that's all."

"Wonder next week."

Mainzer laughed. "That's what I'll do," he said. "See you Saturday."

"Right."

Mainzer left, and Parker waited a few more minutes and then followed him. He went down the stairs, and stopped off at the mezzanine to open the ballroom door and take a look inside. It looked the same as before, with nothing to show it had been breached.

PART THREE

1

TERRY ATKINS of Terry-Kerry Coin Company drove into Indianapolis from Chicago Thursday afternoon in his Pontiac station wagon and arrived at the Clayborn Hotel at about six-thirty. A short dark man of twenty-nine, he and his partner Kerry Christiansen had operated a dealership together for the last five years, clearing between eight and eleven thousand dollars a year apiece. Most of their business was mail order, supplemented almost every weekend by coin conventions such as this one, which they took turns attending.

Crossing the lobby on his way to the desk, Atkins saw three other dealers he knew, got into a brief conversation, and arranged to meet them all in the bar a little later. He went on to the desk, picked up his key, and took the stairs up to the mezzanine to register for the convention at the table that had been set up there by the local coin club. He got his convention badge, attached it to his lapel, and went back downstairs to arrange for a bellboy to bring his things up from the car, now in the basement garage. He had one small suitcase with clothing and such in it, and two large heavy coin cases, the contents of which had a current market value of around thirty-five thousand dollars. These went directly to the Lake Room on the mezzanine, now being used as the security room, where a blue-uniformed Pinkerton guard gave him a claim check which he tucked away in his wallet. He then stopped off at the West Room, down the hall, looking for a friend of his who was in charge of a display of military scrip that would be shown here, but the friend wasn't around so he went on up to his room, showered, changed, and went down to meet the other dealers in the bar.

Thursday at these conventions was always slow and relaxed. The tables wouldn't be set up until tomorrow, so there was very little business to be transacted, except in a desultory way among the dealers themselves. Mostly there was shop talk and drinking and intramural gossip. Atkins had dinner at a downtown restaurant with the other three dealers, made a tentative arrangement to sell one of them a pair of Mexican gold coins tomorrow, and bar-hopped around Indianapolis with them till midnight.

He was up at seven Friday morning, had a quick breakfast in the hotel coffee shop, made his mandatory call to his wife in Chicago, got his coin cases out of the security room, went to his assigned table in the bourse room—number 58, midway along the drape-covered rear wall—and set up his display, stopping from time to time to chat with convention acquaintances who wandered by. There were perhaps two hundred people in the world that he knew fairly well and had never seen anywhere other than at coin conventions; in no other way did they impinge on his private life nor he on theirs.

The bourse opened at ten, but was slow at first. During the morning there was barely a sprinkling of local hobbyists, window-shopping, renewing acquaintances, looking at what was available, but not doing much buying.

Atkins went to lunch at one o'clock with two other dealers. He draped a white cloth over his display table before going, secure in the knowledge that the Pinkerton men and the local coin club's security detail and the dealers at the adjacent tables would among them see to it his table wasn't rifled while he was gone.

In the afternoon he could have spent some time looking at the exhibits in the display rooms, or at the cost of a dollar and a half he could have joined a club-sponsored tour of the city to include the Indianapolis Speedway and its Museum, but a coin convention was primarily business to him, so he went back to the bourse and spent the afternoon sitting in a folding chair behind his assigned table.

Business grew gradually brisker during the afternoon, but there was still plenty of time for small talk with people who came wandering by. These included his friend who had the display of military scrip, and also a local coin dealer named Billy Lebatard. Atkins had no use for Lebatard socially, considering him a bore, but he was a somewhat important dealer, having been able on more than one occasion to fill a specific oddball order from one of Atkins' customers. This time, with no specific business to transact, they chatted together somewhat hesitantly, and Atkins was pleased when they were interrupted by a teenage boy interested in half-cents from the eighteen-thirties.

Around five, as the local people began getting out of work, business picked up fast, and from then till after nine, Atkins almost always had at least one customer browsing at his table. The bourse was to remain open till ten, but by nine-fifteen Atkins was too hungry to stick around any longer, so he draped the cloth over his table, joined three other dealers, and they went out to a restaurant, followed by another night of bar-hopping.

The others seemed ready to go all night, but Atkins had had enough by twelve-thirty, and went back to the hotel by himself. He rang for the elevator, but nothing happened for quite a while, so he went up the stairs. There was a Pinkerton man sitting at a card table near the staircase on the mezzanine floor. The ballroom and security room and display room doors were all closed. A second Pinkerton man was walking around the open mezzanine, strolling along, looking over the railing down at the lobby.

Halfway up the next flight, Atkins came across Billy Lebatard again, this time with a short, thin, older man who carried that inevitable symbol of the tourist, a camera hanging from a thong around his neck. The older man also carried a small sketch pad and a pencil, and had apparently been making some kind of drawing. The two of them hadn't been going anywhere, just standing in the corner of the landing between the mezzanine and the second floor. When Atkins came into view, Lebatard acted very flustered, but the older man paid no attention to Atkins at all. Atkins said hello to Lebatard and went on upstairs, wondering vaguely at Lebatard's reaction. He wondered idly if Lebatard might after all be homosexual, and had picked up—or been picked up by—an older man of the same type. Lebatard definitely wasn't very masculine in his looks or actions. But it was none of Atkins' business, and by the time he'd reached his room he'd forgotten about it.

Saturday was much busier than Friday. Atkins took a short fast lunch at two o'clock, but otherwise stayed at his table from ten o'clock opening till the bourse closed at eight o'clock for the banquet.

The Saturday banquet was an integral part of these conventions, where the social and hobby aspects reached their peak. Awards were given at the banquet for the best exhibits in the display rooms. Speeches were made, and entertainment had to be sat through. The majority of convention-goers attended the banquet, not including Terry Atkins, who was too business-oriented to take much pleasure in the sight of hobbyists getting together to laugh too much at in-jokes, to give each other prizes, and to eat chicken and peas and ice cream. Atkins and a few like-minded dealer friends went instead to eat steak at a good restaurant and then to sit around a cozy bar and drink happily together. They told each other cheerfully that they were doing business, the stock was moving. It was a good convention. Nothing spectacular, nothing unusual, pretty much the expected sort of thing, but all in all a good convention.

They drank to it.

2

LEMPKE STOOD in the kitchen of Billy Lebatard's house and watched the water not boiling. What he really wanted was Jim Beam on the rocks, straight, in a tall glass, with the bottle and some more ice cubes handy, but he'd learned years ago—decades ago—that you don't drink the same night you go out to pull a job, not if you want to stay outside and healthy. Afterwards he could drink all he wanted, could and would, but right now he'd have to make do with tea. If the water would just boil.

Billy Lebatard stuck his head in the doorway and said, "Parker wants to know where you are."

"One minute," Lempke said. It was late Saturday night, the clock on the kitchen wall reading eleven thirty-seven, and it was past time for the meeting to begin. But Lempke's stomach was knotting up and he was going to have to put something inside there before he could go into the dining room and sit down at that table and take part the way he was supposed to, so he said, "Tell him just one minute. I'll be right there." And glared impatiently at the pot of water on the stove.

Billy said reluctantly, "Okay, I'll tell him," but he didn't go anywhere. Instead, he leaned farther into the kitchen and whispered, "You won't say anything, will you?"

"I told you I won't," Lempke said.

"I don't want ..." Billy looked troubled, and made vague gestures.

"I know what you want," Lempke said sharply.

Billy looked startled, and then hurt. Wordlessly, he turned and went away. Lempke was already sorry at having lost his temper with the poor boy, but there was nothing to do about it now. Besides, the water was finally boiling. He poured it into the cup, where the teabag was already waiting, and then waited again, this time for the tea to steep, which shouldn't take more than a minute.

The thing about Billy, he shouldn't act like that. Not so upset, the way he got at the hotel last night when a dealer he knew came up the stairs, or the way he was now, asking Lempke over and over not to tell Parker how he'd gotten rattled at the hotel. For himself, Lempke thought, there was some excuse; he was an old man, he'd taken a fall, his wind and nerves and everything else were starting to go. But for Billy, young and smart, there was no excuse at all. Lempke had taken to the boy from their first meeting, and hated to have to admit to himself that Billy Lebatard was simply a coward. He was almost like a father saddled with a disappointing son.

August Lempke had no children of his own, though he'd been married twice. The first marriage had taken place when he was twenty-three, seven years after his first big-time heist. He had a house in Atlantic City in those days, he played the swell along the boardwalk, and that was where he met Marge. They fell in love, they married, and seven months later he made the mistake of telling her how he made his living. She went straight to the law, and he got clear by a whisker. She didn't waste any time about divorces, but got herself an annulment instead, and for the next twenty-two years he lived the bachelor's life, until twelve years ago he'd married Cathy Russell, widow of Cam Russell, one of the best of the old-time juggers, a man who'd known more about bank vaults than most bankers but who'd been shot down by a rookie cop on a job in Wilmington Delaware that had gone sour all the way. Lempke and Cathy had had six good years together before he took his fall, in Rhode Island, but she'd died—heart trouble—while he was inside, and when he'd come out at last a few months back there was nobody to greet him in the sunshine, no address written on a slip of paper in his pocket. He knew nothing except the life of the heister, knew no one except other pros in the business. He was broke and alone and for both those reasons he needed a score. And because he was old and had been out of circulation he knew the score would have to originate with him; no one else would be going out of their way to include him on any string.

He started looking around among the people he knew, and a general heavy named Bainum sent him to Billy Lebatard. Bainum had knocked over a coin dealer fingered by Lebatard once, and though there hadn't been much profit in it, a similar sort of job might at least set Lempke up with a new stake. So Lempke had looked Billy up, had found him to be a grown-up orphan, a man living alone in his dead folks' house, a little boy still behind the adult façade, and Lempke had been ripe to play a paternal role.

The idea of knocking over the whole convention had come from Billy, or maybe from Claire, whom Lempke had been wary of from the beginning. When the idea came along Lempke had got hold of Jack French and Parker, and all at once the job had been taken over by Parker, a man who put the stamp of his own cold style on every heist he worked. Parker was cold and solid, and Lempke knew it was only that coldness that was keeping the rest of them together. Billy wanted to fall apart under the pressure, he wanted that the way a torture victim wants to die. Lempke himself felt the weakness of age and worry lapping at the edges of his mind. Otto Mainzer, a crazy man, a destroyer, was being held in check by the authority of Parker.

All he had to do, Lempke told himself, was hold on. Parker was running things, and doing a good job of it, and all Lempke had to do was obey orders, act the way his own training and experience told him to act, and everything would come out fine.

"Lempke."

He looked around, startled. Parker was in the doorway, looking at him. "Oh!" Lempke said, "I'm coming now."

Parker turned away, and Lempke hurriedly took the teabag out of the cup, threw it away, and carried the cup into the dining room.

The rest of them were sitting around the table there, Parker at one end and Billy at the other, Otto Mainzer and Mike Carlow on one side, Claire and the empty chair for Lempke on the other. Lempke slid into his chair, putting his teacup down, and Parker said, "Lempke, you looked it over last night. Tell us about it."

"Right," Lempke said, and sipped at his tea, but it was still too hot. He put the cup down again and said, "The setup's no problem."

"We made sure of everything," Billy said, looking around for a gold star.

Lempke said, "Shut up, Billy." He knew how to do this sort of thing, his professionalism was still of use to him here, and so right now he had no patience with Billy. To the table at large he said, "There's five Pinkertons on duty after the ballroom closes. One in the ballroom itself and one in the security room, both of them with the doors closed and locked. One in the main display room, also closed and locked. One on plant at a table near the elevators and stairs, and one roaming. The roamer checks the three locked in the rooms every hour on the hour. The night men go to work at ten, when the ballroom closes, and their relief comes on at six. But that could be different tonight, because the ballroom closes at eight."

Parker said, "How do they work the hour check?"

"The roamer knocks on the door, the man inside opens it, they say a few words back and forth. It didn't look like they had passwords or signals or anything, but we couldn't get close enough to be sure. At the two-o'clock check, the roamer brought the inside men sandwiches and coffee. They were delivered from an all-night place across the street from the hotel."

Lempke reached over and got a manila envelope from where Billy had put it down in front of himself. "I got some pictures," he said. "And some sketches. So you can see how it works."

The pictures and sketches were passed around, and then Parker said, "This one from the lobby, shooting up, showing the ballroom doors. Where were you when you took that?"

"Green sofa near the florist stand."

"From there you can see the roamer make his check?"

"Right."

"What about contact between security room and ballroom?"

"We used binoculars from sidewalk level across the street," Lempke said. "The angle was bad, but I'm almost positive that door was open. Anyway, it would make sense, the two men on duty there get to talk to one another."

"We'll assume it's open," Parker said. "And the best time to hit is two o'clock, when they get the sandwiches and coffee. They'll both be in the same room, eating together. Lempke, when you're in that green sofa, can you be seen from the street?"

"Sure. Through the main lobby doors."

"Good. Claire, you start sitting in that lobby at quarter to two. As soon as both those guards get their food, you give the signal."

Claire said, "How?"

"You sit with your legs crossed. The signal is, you switch the legs."

Claire smiled and nodded. "That's easy," she said.

"You stick around another ten minutes or so," Parker told her, "and then you come up with the rest of us."

"All right."

Lempke sipped at his tea, which was now at just the right temperature. The tea was warming in his stomach, and the stolid impersonality of Parker was the best kind of reassurance. Lempke felt the pre-heist jitters fading away, felt the old calmness and confidence coming back at last, out of mothballs, out of the past. He hadn't felt sure of himself since the walls of that Rhode Island prison had closed around him, and it was like meeting an old friend after years of separation to feel this stronger self coming back into his body, taking over the controls again after such a long time.

Lempke smiled to himself. He was going to be all right after all.

Parker was saying to Carlow, "You get the truck there by ten to two. You and Otto set up where I showed you, and then you get where you can see Claire through the lobby doors. I'll be at the tour office window. When she gives you the sign, you light a cigarette and walk back to the truck. Otto, as soon as things are set up by the truck you come upstairs with the rest of us. I'll have the door rigged."

Grinning, Mainzer said, "I'll be there."

"We'll give ourselves fifty minutes," Parker said. "What we don't get within that time we leave. Billy, you got that chart for us?"

"Oh, sure," Billy said, jumping to his feet. "I had it, I had—Lempke's got it, in the envelope."

"Relax, Billy," Lempke said, and handed over the chart. It was done with ruled ink lines on a plain sheet of white paper.

Billy explained the chart at great length, but Lempke didn't bother to listen, partly because Billy had already explained it to him earlier and partly because the chart was self-explanatory. It was a drawing of the ballroom, showing all the display tables, numbered. Some of the numbers were circled in red, and these were the tables to be concentrated on. Of the hundred and three tables in the ballroom, thirty-seven were marked with red.

When Billy was finally done, Parker looked around at them all and said, "We can do this with fewer men, it'll just mean we get less of the available goods. Lebatard's the only indispensable man. Anybody else want out?"

There was silence at the table, until Lempke felt Parker's eyes on him. He had been feeling so good for the last few minutes that it hadn't occurred to him at first that Parker, in offering this last out, had been talking mostly to him, but now that it did he smiled broadly and shook his head, saying, "Not me, Parker. I heard the gun and I'm in the race."

Parker kept looking at him, and Lempke met his eyes. He *knew* he was all right, so it didn't matter.

And Parker saw it, too, Lempke knew it, when Parker's expression changed, became easier, and he said, "Hello, Lempke."

3

THE NIGHTS were always the dullest.

Fred Hoffman, fifty-four years of age, had been a Pinkerton employee since the end of the Second World War, when he'd been honorably discharged from the Army, where he'd served in the Military Police, and in all the years of his employ he had never fired his pistol anywhere except on the practice range, and in fact had never so much as heard a pistol fired anywhere but on the range. Not that he minded, most of the time. He wasn't all that anxious to get involved in shoot-outs. He considered his presence in the blue Pinkerton uniform to be in the nature of a deterrent rather than a challenge. If there was a disturbance, any sort of disturbance, he had already failed in his function, and then he would have to fall back on his secondary function of peacemaker. Up till now, he had never failed in the primary function, and had experienced over twenty years of peacefulness.

Which was all well and good, and what he was paid for, but sometimes—and particularly on the night shifts—he found himself with a real hankering for action, for an end to peace, for something to *happen*.

Well, nothing ever did. And nothing would tonight, either. Hoffman walked up and down the cloth-shrouded aisles, surrounded by hundreds of thousands of dollars' worth of coins, maybe millions of dollars' worth, and nothing happened, except that every now and then George Dolnick came in from the security room next door and they threw the bull a little, and every hour Pat Schuyler came knocking on the door and Hoffman opened it and they exchanged the code words that meant everything was—invariably—all right.

Hoffman also liked to look out the window and watch the traffic go by, but as the night grew later the traffic grew lighter, and by the time of Pat Schuyler's one-o'clock check there was practically nothing happening out in the street. Still, it was sometimes more pleasant to look out at the empty street than in at the rows of tables all covered with white cloths, like long lumpy rows of slabs in a futuristic morgue.

Hoffman was looking out the window at about ten before two when the power-and-light truck arrived and came to a stop almost exactly outside the window. Hoffman watched with bored interest as two men in work jumpers climbed out of the truck and set up barriers around a manhole and then took the manhole cover off. It only took them a few minutes to get set up, moving right along, but then nothing happened at all. One of the two men, the larger one, went away down the street to the right, out of Hoffman's vision, and the other one went down to the left and sort of stood around on the sidewalk there, under the hotel marquee, as though he had nothing on earth to do.

Union labor, Hoffman thought, and nodded to himself. He might be an employee himself, but he was down on the kind of union you read about in the papers these days; always going on strike for more money or fewer hours, but never lifting a finger to see that the members did an honest day's work for all those wages.

Hoffman kept watching, wondering just how long those two would dawdle around, probably getting time and a half for being on the job so late, but when the code knock came at the door at two o'clock the one under the marquee still hadn't moved and the other one still hadn't come back.

Hoffman opened the door and Pat Schuyler was there, holding a small brown paper bag. They exchanged the no-trouble phrases and Schuyler handed over the paper bag, saying, "We got us a looker down in the lobby tonight."

"Is that right?"

"You can see her from here."

Hoffman looked past Schuyler, at an angle down through the railing into the lobby, and nodded. "So she is," he said. "Now what do you suppose she's waiting for?"

"No old fogies like us," said Schuyler, "I can tell you that."

"You speak for yourself," Hoffman told him, and they grinned at each other, and Hoffman shut the door.

When he turned, George Dolnick had come in from the security room, carrying his own brown paper bag. Dolnick said, "Another exciting night, eh, Fred?"

"I don't think I can stand the pace," Hoffman said.

They went over to the small cleared table near the windows and sat down. They opened their bags and a harsh voice said, "Freeze."

Hoffman looked around, and a lot of masked men were coming through the wall.

4

OTTO MAINZER felt good. He felt tall, strong, smart, and capable. The Colt Trooper .357 Magnum in his right hand was as small and light as a peanut, but it was his lightning-fast snake, his poison dart. He moved on the balls of his feet, coming in fast behind Parker, through the gap in the wall and through the heavy drapes, moving to the left as Parker moved to the right, seeing Lempke out of the corner of his eye, coming in third, moving along the wall after Parker.

The two private fuzz were sitting at a table near the window, their open mouths full of food. They'd turned their heads at Parker's barked one-word command, but after that neither of them had moved a muscle.

The mask restricted Mainzer's vision just slightly, cutting down his peripheral vision so that he had to move slowly, his left hand out to the side testing for tables or other obstructions. While Parker and Lempke were moving along the drapes to the front wall, Mainzer headed away at a sharp angle to the left, going down the aisle between the display tables till he came to the cross-aisle halfway down, then going across to the other side of the room and heading back toward the fuzz.

Now he and Parker were at two points of a triangle, with the Pinks at the third, and Lempke could go in and disarm them without obscuring everybody's line of fire at once. Mainzer stood with cocked hip, smiling inside his mask, while Lempke stripped the Pinks of their hardware, putting the guns on the table with the half-eaten sandwiches.

Lempke then backed away toward the open door of the security room, motioning at the cops to follow him. They did, both of them looking shaky and disgusted with themselves. Mainzer followed them into the other room, while Parker stayed out in the ballroom.

Lempke had rope and tape. As Mainzer stood guard, Lempke put the fuzz down on the floor, tied them, and taped their mouths. Then they went back outside and Lempke pulled off his mask, saying, "Hot in there."

Parker already had his off. "Go get Billy," he said.

"Right." Lempke hurried away across the room.

Mainzer still had his mask on. He liked the feel of it. He said, "There's a couple suitcases in the other room."

"We'll ask Billy. You want to take that off before you go outside."

Mainzer felt sudden embarrassment and anger, as though he'd been caught doing something dirty. He felt his face grow red inside the mask, making it impossible for him to take it off yet. "I will," he said stiffly, trying to hide both the embarrassment and the anger. "Don't worry about me."

Lempke came back through the hole with Billy, who was white with terror and stumbling over his own feet. Billy stood just inside the drape, looking around big-eyed, and whispered, "Where are they?"

"We chopped them up," Mainzer said, feeling a surge of contempt for this soft fool, "and put the pieces in suitcases."

Parker said, "Let's get started. Billy, where's the chart?"

Billy had to fumble around in pockets, but he finally did come up with the chart and they went to work. Billy and Lempke packed, Parker carried the full cases through the wall to the tour office, and Mainzer brought them downstairs to Carlow, who stowed them away in the truck.

Mainzer didn't remove the mask until he was out of the ballroom, just before making his first trip to the street. In the darkness of the tour office he tugged the mask off and shoved it into a pocket. He could feel his face still flaming red, but in the darkness it might go unnoticed.

He kept thinking of things he should have said to Parker, things he still could say. Every trip up and down the stairs his mind was full of cutting remarks, clever answers, tough challenges; he mouthed them as he went along, glowering.

From time to time he would run into Parker in the tour office, the both of them arriving there simultaneously, Parker with more filled cases, Mainzer empty-handed, and every time he was on the verge of saying something, just at the edge of making an issue, but it never quite happened. He told himself it was better not to start anything now. They were working on a tight schedule, too tight for anything extraneous. Afterwards they could have it out, just the two of them. Parker was too much of a hard-nose, he was going around looking for a broken head, and, Mainzer figured, he might be just the boy to give it to him, one way or another.

At the other end of his route was Carlow, and there too a tight-lipped truce was in effect. The truce had more violent overtones here, though, because both of them were aware of its existence. Mainzer and Carlow spoke to one another only when it was absolutely necessary, and then in the fewest possible number of syllables. Driving downtown together in the truck they hadn't said a word to one another, and both knew they were only waiting for the job to be finished before they got down to their private disagreement.

What the disagreement was neither of them particularly knew or cared. They rubbed each other the wrong way, they were enemies, they were waiting for the communal task to be finished and then they would be at each other's throats—that was all they knew and all they had to know.

Mainzer was not entirely honoring this truce, finding small, indirect ways to irritate Carlow. Like the placement of the coin cases; it would have been just as easy, and more sensible, for him to put them on the tailgate when bringing them out to the truck, but instead he ostentatiously put them down in the street directly behind the truck, leaving the smaller and lighter Carlow the job of lifting them up and putting them inside. He did this the first three trips downstairs, but on the fourth trip Carlow was already in the truck, way back in the darkness at the end, and when Mainzer put the cases down in the street Carlow called, with heavy sarcasm, "In here, Tarzan."

Mainzer smiled thinly, "Sure thing, pal," he said, picked one of the cases up, set it on the truck bed, and gave it a hard push toward Carlow, trying to knock him off his feet with it Carlow jumped to the side, the case thudded into the ones already stacked in place, and Carlow put his hand inside his overall pocket saying, "Send the other one that way, buster."

"Whatever you want, pal," Mainzer said, but he pushed the second case in more gently than the first, and after that he put the cases inside the truck instead of outside.

It was on his way up after his fifth trip that he ran into Parker's bitch, also on the way in. Claire, her name was, and he had to admit she was a good-looking piece. But probably frigid.

The educated ones with the cool good looks and the clothes right out of the fashion magazines, they were the frigid ones, nine times out of ten. The only ones that wanted it were the dumb fatties, and they were the ones that Mainzer had no taste for. Because of this, he very rarely had any sort of relations with a woman, and when he did have anything going it was always short-lived, the woman invariably turning out to be either dumb or frigid. He didn't know why that was so, or how other men got around the problem, but on the other hand he didn't care a hell of a lot either. They were better things to do with the male body than laying it on some woman. The big times in his life had mostly happened at night, but never in bed.

Like stomping Carlow, for instance. He was going to enjoy that. And Parker, too. In fact, with Parker he'd enjoy it even more, because it would be tougher to work out.

In any case, Mainzer wasn't primarily a ladies' man. Still, he had an image to maintain and a view of life to re-confirm, which was why he'd greeted Claire on first meeting her with a bluntly phrased suggestion, and why, on running into her again at the office building doorway now, he said, "Change your mind yet, honey?"

She gave him a look of cool contempt—which he knew to be phony—and went on ahead of him into the building. He followed her up the stairs, watching the way her hips moved. He thought of other things he might say to her, but he kept silent. He also thought briefly of grabbing her in the hallway, giving her a quickie in payment for that look of contempt, but he put that idea out of his mind right away. He'd tried something like that once, years ago when he was younger and thought all women wanted it, thought frigidity was always a fake, thought all you had to do was climb aboard and they'd sigh, "Oh, yes, I *do* want it!" Instead of which, he'd suddenly found his arms full of grizzly bear. That little bitch had been the worst, dirtiest, most vicious and violent fighter he'd ever come up against in his life. She bit, clawed, scratched, kicked, gouged, butted, kneed, elbowed and generally tried to rip his skin off. He'd finally had to knock her out, in self-defense, and he never did get into her pants, though when he'd looked at her lying there on that floor unconscious he'd had half a mind to go ahead and do it anyway. The thought that she might wake up halfway through had stopped him.

And the memory of her had stopped him on every similar occasion since then, including now. He followed Claire on into the Diablo Tours office, and when she bent to go through the hole in the wall the only desire he had was to kick her for a field goal.

Until Claire's arrival, things had been slow for Mainzer, with pauses after every trip while he waited for two more cases to be gotten ready, but now that Claire was helping pack it went faster, and Mainzer moved constantly back and forth between tour office and truck. In the ballroom, he knew, Lempke and Claire and Billy were all packing the coin cases, while Parker sometimes packed and sometimes carried the full cases out of the office.

Mainzer kept track, and by ten minutes to three he had made twenty-seven round trips. With two cases each time, that meant fifty-four cases of coins already stowed in the truck. Going into the building for the twenty-eighth time, about to start up the stairs, Mainzer sensed movement in the darkness behind him, and turned. The piece of pipe glanced off the side of his head and pounded onto his shoulder, bringing blinding pain. He made a sound high in the back of his throat, sagged, weaved, and the indistinct figure in front of him swung again. This time he saw the pipe a fraction of an inch in front of his eyes, coming with the speed of fury.

5

MIKE CARLOW wasn't entirely sure which he liked least, Mainzer or this cruddy truck, but he thought it was probably the truck. He hadn't liked it when he first saw it, covered with canvas, in the backyard of Lebatard's house, and he'd liked it even less after he and that bastard Mainzer had taken the canvas off, and he'd begun to really despise it once he was behind the wheel and had the rotten thing in some kind of motion. He didn't like the transmission, he didn't like the engine, he didn't like the springs, he didn't like the seat or the steering wheel or the tires, and most of all he didn't like the idea of pushing this orange lemon around the city streets with a million dollars' worth of hot coins stowed away in the back.

A vehicle, to Mike Carlow, was something that got you from point A to point B in one second flat, regardless of the distance between. This was the ideal, not yet attained either in Detroit or Europe, and Carlow judged everything with wheels and an engine on how close it came to reaching the ideal. And this truck Parker had given him to drive was the bottom of the barrel, was further from the ideal than anything else he could think of, with the possible exception of a power lawn mower.

Carlow was a racing driver, and in his high-school days had pushed a lot of clunkers around a lot of stock-car tracks. While still a teenager he'd designed a racing car with a center of gravity guaranteed to be unaffected by the amount of gasoline in the gas tank, because there wasn't any gas tank; the car was built around a frame of hollow aluminum tubing, which would hold the fuel supply. When someone he showed the idea to objected that it might be insanely dangerous to build a car in which the driver was completely surrounded by gasoline, he'd said, "So what?" And had lived his life from the same point of view ever since.

If racing cars didn't cost so damn much to design and build and care for Mike Carlow wouldn't from time to time be reduced to driving abortions like this stinking truck. He worked on jobs like this maybe once a year, less if he could afford it, and only to raise enough cash to support his automobiles. Sure, he could sell out to one of the big companies, be in essence nothing more than a test pilot for them, trying their engineers' bright new ideas in racing cars financed by them, owned by them, and merely driven by him, but that wasn't his idea of racing. Any car he drove had to be *his* car, and his designs were still as wild as the track officials would permit. Because of this, and because he was one of the most aggressive drivers in the business, he had racked up more than his share of cars, leaving himself with marks of his occupation all over his body. More important, to his way of thinking, he'd also occasionally reduced thousands of dollars' worth of automobile to a hundred dollars' worth of scrap, and every time that happened he either had to dip into the kitty if there was one or hire himself out to people like Parker and Lempke again, to take them safely and quickly away from the scene of a score. Or to drive some piece of garbage like this improbable truck.

As for Otto Mainzer, the bastard was a bastard, that was all there was to say about him. As long as Mainzer kept his rotten personality within bounds Carlow would control himself, but once this job was over if Mainzer wanted to go on being cute Carlow would be happy to bend a tire iron over his head. It wouldn't be the first time he'd stretched out a bruiser who thought he could have it over Carlow because of the difference in their sizes, and it might not be the last, but Carlow thought it would probably be the one he'd enjoy the most.

In the meantime, tonight's work was mostly dull. The highlight had been watching Parker's woman cross her legs; from then on, the night had been downhill. All he had to do was stand around behind the truck a lot, looking into the open manhole and making believe he was a power-and-light worker, and when Mainzer brought him more of the boodle he had to go into the truck and stash it.

Only once in the last hour had he seen a police car, and that had gone on by him without a glance. Other than that, traffic had been so light as to be almost nonexistent, and pedestrians going by on the sidewalk were as rare as dodo eggs. Occasionally Mainzer had to wait out of sight in the doorway while groups of conventioneers, most of them carrying cargoes of alcohol, straggled by and into the hotel, but these delays were never long. Carlow did his work methodically, spent most of his free time thinking about his tentative plans for the next car he wanted to build, and when at ten minutes to three the man in the topcoat and hat walked over and stood in front of him Carlow at first didn't even see the gun in his hand. He said, "What's up, buddy?" thinking the guy was going to ask directions or something like that.

But the guy said, "You are. Let's take a walk." And motioned with the gun.

Then Carlow saw it, and a feeling like ice water ran down the middle of his back. He looked at the guy's face again, and he just didn't look like law. Carlow said, "I'm easy. No need to get excited." And moved his arms out from his sides, so he wouldn't look as though he was reaching for anything.

"That's the way to be, all right," said the other. "Let's go inside."

"Sure."

The guy wanted him to go into the office building. Carlow left the truck and walked across the sidewalk and pushed open the door, the man with the gun coming along behind him.

Inside, Carlow saw the dim form of Mainzer lying on the floor near the foot of the stairs. *I'm going to get it, too,* he thought, and then pain came curving in a bright hard flash around both sides of his head and turned the world to white darkness.

6

BILLY LEBATARD felt like Judas Iscariot. He stood there in the brightly lighted bourse room, packing coins into case after case, and though in a small way he did feel the excitement and the thrill that he thought natural to a scene like this, what he mostly felt was sick and rotten and miserable and the worst kind of Benedict Arnold.

Because this was much worse than the other times, the two or three times when money had been short and he had helped professional criminals to rob coin dealers. Well, not *helped* exactly. He'd merely pointed out in each case a good subject, and told the robbers what they needed to know about their victim's movements, and then afterward he'd brought the stolen coins for something less than half of their retail value.

Of course, no matter how you looked at it, those times had been just the same as this one, just as bad, just as crooked. But this one *felt* worse. Mostly, probably, it was because those other times the victims had been individual dealers he hadn't really known all that well, men he'd only met a few times around the convention circuit, and this time the primary victims were going to be the members of the Indianapolis Coin Association, the host club for this convention. And they were people Billy had known for years, people who had befriended him, had invited him to their homes, had accepted him and welcomed him and thought of him as their friend.

Billy Lebatard well knew the value of friendship. He'd been a shy and lonely child, and at times it had seemed as though his entire life would be lonely, and numismatics had saved him. Fellow hobbyists share something important to them which the outside world considers unimportant and frivolous, so that in a small way all hobbyists are social outcasts; a true social outcast can become less noticeable in their midst.

Billy was the younger of two boys, his father being a druggist with his own small store down in Beach Grove. The older boy, Dick, had gone off to be a Greenwich Village beatnik at an early age, but Billy had been more the stay-at-home type. The family had assumed that he would be going to college, but when two months after high-school graduation his mother and father both died in a bus accident on their way home from a druggists' convention in Columbus, Ohio, Billy suddenly discovered he had no true desire to go to college, nor to do much of anything else. He had inherited the house in Mars Hill and the drugstore and about twenty-two thousand dollars; he was eighteen years old; and he had no ambition. He sold the drugstore, split the inheritance with Dick, continued to live at home, and devoted more and more of his time to his hobby of coin collecting.

The transition from hobbyist to dealer had been gradual, and he'd already been a dealer in a small way months before he first took a table at a coin convention. His business had expanded until he could usually make a living from it, with only those few slumps when he'd taken to fencing stolen goods. Until Claire had come into his life he'd had neither desire nor need for a great deal of money.

Claire showed up because Dick had a wife out there in New York, and the wife had an airline pilot brother, who a couple of years ago had chosen to live in the Indianapolis area. For some reason Dick had suggested that the pilot look Billy up, which he did, bringing his good-looking wife Claire along, but Billy and the pilot hadn't hit it off together at all, and Billy saw neither of them again until over a year later, when Claire called to ask if he could recommend a local undertaker.

When he heard that the pilot was dead, something stirred in Billy's mind, and the most violent physical lust he'd ever experienced shook him like a fox shaking a rabbit. He craved Claire, craved her beyond rationality. For as long as possible he hid this craving behind a façade of helpfulness, and when at last he did make his shaky, clumsy, terrified proposition she had cut him dead with such cold viciousness that he retreated at once to helpfulness again, trying to make believe that nothing had ever been said on either side.

It was a while after that that Claire had come to him and told him she needed seventy thousand dollars. She wouldn't tell him why, and she wouldn't make any real promises, but the implication was very clear that if Billy could come up with the needed money his earlier proposition would be reconsidered in a much kindlier light.

And now here he was, stealing other people's coins, surrounded by hard, violent, self-assured men, betraying all the people who had ever befriended him. At the other end of the room was Claire, who had never even allowed him to kiss her, and moving back and forth was the man named Parker, who Billy was sure had actually been to bed with Claire.

But he didn't care. He told himself he didn't care, not about that, nor about the betrayal of his friends, nor about anything else. Soon this would all be over, the robbery finished. Parker gone, the money coming in, and then everything would be all right. Claire wasn't going to get a penny until after she'd been in Billy's bed, he'd promised himself that, and he was going to stick to it.

In the meantime, the work was almost finished. Billy was hot inside his coat, perspiring, but he didn't dare take it off because he'd disobeyed Parker's orders. His gun, a chrome-handled Colt Commander .38 automatic, was in its holster under his left arm. He'd bought it before attending his second convention as a dealer, he'd worn it almost constantly for a while, he still wore it at every possible excuse, and it seemed to him that tonight's work required its presence more than any other time before this. So he had it on, Parker or no Parker, and he also had his coat on, and inside it he was perspiring.

But it was all almost over. Parker himself came over and said, "It's ten to three. When you're done with that case, carry it down to the truck. We're clearing out."

"Good," Billy said, and meant it. He'd been more nervous than he liked to admit, and he was glad it was coming to an end.

It only took him a minute more to finish packing this case, so he would be leaving before any of the others, Parker or Lempke or Claire. He picked up the case, which seemed to weigh a ton, and carried it over to the hole in the wall, where he had to put it down, go backwards through the hole, and then pull the case through after himself.

The tour office was very dark, after the brightly lit bourse room. Billy stood there a few seconds, waiting for his eyes to adjust, and then he saw Jack French standing over by the door, wearing hat and topcoat.

Billy was surprised and confused, but not frightened. "French!" he said, "What are you doing here?"

"Come over here," French said, and motioned, and Billy saw he was holding a gun in his hand. Billy, without thinking, dropped the case and reached for his gun.

He died astonished.

7

UNTIL SHE heard the sound of the shot Claire had thought there was nothing left for her to find out. But then she heard it, muffled and indistinct but unmistakable, and she thought, "Somebody just died." And her knees gave way. She slid down sideways through the air, glancing off the edge of the table she'd been clearing, hitting the floor hard on her left shoulder, rolling onto her back and then just lying there, staring up at the ceiling.

She never actually lost consciousness. But she had no strength in her body, no will in her mind, no control over her emotions. Inside, she was gibbering with terror and guilt. Reality had just hit her a paralyzing blow.

Because it wasn't a game, this venture she was on. Nothing in life was a game, nothing, and she hadn't known that until this second.

It had seemed a game when she was growing up, and the name of the game was let-'em-have-less-than-they-want, and if she lost that game sometimes what did it matter? And later on the name of the game was glamorous-life, and even when Ed died it didn't really change things, because he had died hundreds of miles away on some mountainside, his death as glamorous as his life, his death merely another way of playing the game.

And when the clod Billy came snuffling around, just at the time she learned how little Ed had left her, that she wasn't merely broke but actually in debt, the name of the game became confidence, and that was just another way to have the glamorous life and to give them less than they wanted. Claire the con woman, romantic and elusive.

The number seventy thousand had come out of the air. Actually she owed about eighteen hundred dollars and was prepared to skip out on that, but Billy had done some boasting about how much he had salted away and it had seemed to Claire she'd do better at the game of life with a healthy stake, so she'd given him a mysterious song and dance, a couple of half-promises, and it turned out Billy didn't have that sort of cash on hand.

But Claire could already taste the money. With a lot of money she could leave Indianapolis, travel, see a lot more of the good life that Ed had been her entrée to, while without the money she was stuck in this town, she'd have to hunt around in too much of a hurry for a second husband, the game would turn sour.

The transition from Billy's called bluff to this bourse room on this Saturday night had been gradual, with the game slowly becoming one that was played for keeps, but still being a game, always a game. So she'd given Parker the same seventy-thousand story as Billy, but something about the remote strength and cold self-assurance of Parker had gotten through to her and she'd given him other things, too, that Billy had never gotten. Which simply made the game more interesting.

Until the shot.

It was as though a layer of mud had been abruptly washed away from the inscription on a tomb, so that she could suddenly see words she had never suspected the existence of before, telling her a truth too unbearable to support. So she had fallen, and was lying here, and in all the jumble that her mind had turned into only one picture kept returning and returning: Ed, broken open like a sausage, smeared across that rocky mountainside. Inside, in a quiet corner away from the panic and the guilt and the chaos, she began for the first time to mourn her husband.

Parker came into her line of vision, a gun in his hand, but he was only a black shape between her and the white ceiling. He spoke, harsh and quick, and the words might as well have been Swahili. She wanted to say to him, "Help me escape the responsibility. Don't let them make me pay. I didn't know how it was." But she couldn't organize words, couldn't find the strength or the method.

Parker leaned down and slapped her face, very hard, so that her head rocked, and afterward the whole side of her face began to sting and burn, the feeling getting worse and worse. She closed her eyes, knowing she deserved it but wishing it wouldn't happen.

This time when he spoke she understood the words. "On your feet," he said. "Now. On your feet."

She didn't move, and he slapped her again, on the other side of the face, even harder, and she burst violently into tears, as though she'd been weeping for an hour already. As though someone would turn on a television set and the picture would show someone who has been crying for a long while without letup.

But Parker wouldn't change. His voice cut through her own sounds, telling her again to get on her feet, and only the new fear of his hand made it possible for her to nod her head and move her arms and actually start to get up.

He didn't help. She pulled herself up with the table beside her, and when she was vertical he said, "We're getting out of here. Stay with me."

"Don't show me any pictures," she said, because it seemed to her that Parker was some kind of judge, and he had pictures of who had been killed when the shot was fired, and he was going to show them to her, and she wouldn't be able to bear it.

"Stay with me," he said, ignoring her, and started away.

She moved after him, hurrying on shaky legs, her mind still a jumble, and ahead of her Lempke came backing out of the wall and turned around and his head was all bloody. "French," he said, wide-eyed, and fell down.

Claire began to scream.

PART FOUR

1

THE SCREAM tore it.

Parker looked around, and the job was sour, it was dead, it was in pieces around him. Billy Lebatard had to be dead. Lempke was maybe dead, maybe dying, maybe just unconscious. Carlow and Mainzer had to be already taken out of the play. French had come back in to hijack the operation, and was blocking the exit through the tour office.

There'd only been the one shot. Lebatard must have brought his goddam gun after all, that's why he kept his coat on. French was a pro, he wouldn't be in a hurry to do any shooting, so Lebatard must have forced his hand. Then he'd slugged Lempke when Lempke poked his head through the hole in the wall, but French was a little shaky himself now and he didn't manage to get Lempke right. He had got him enough to put him out, but not before showing himself to Claire and setting her off like a siren.

Would French clear out, or would he stay a few minutes in the tour office? It depended how rattled Lebatard had made him, and Parker didn't want to take the chance. There was no safe way to go through the wall.

Which left the other route, through the hotel. They were alerted out there now anyway, because of Claire's scream, so they'd have to be contended with no matter which way Parker went out, but it was still a bad alternative. Out, and down the stairs, and through the lobby, and onto the street.

Parker wasted no time thinking about it. He looked around, saw the situation, and moved. He grabbed Claire by the arm and said, "Come on. You brought me in, you can bring me out."

She came along as docile as a zombie. After the one scream she'd gone silent, her face chalk-white, and Parker doubted there was any comprehension at all behind those eyes right now.

Not that he cared. To do her part she wouldn't have to think.

There was already pounding at the double doors, and a voice calling. Parker dragged Claire along behind him into the security room, shut the intervening door, and went over to the hall door. "When I open this," he said, "you walk out there. Move when I push, stop when I pull."

She didn't respond, but he thought she probably had the idea. He opened the door, stepped behind Claire, grabbed a handful of her sweater at the small of her back, and pushed slightly. She walked.

Two Pinkerton men were to the left, hammering on the ballroom doors. Another Pink was at the far end of the mezzanine, having come out of the display room down there to see what was going on.

Parker shouted, "Everybody keep cool!" He started backing away toward the stairs, keeping Claire in front of him. She moved with him, doll-like and obedient.

One of the Pinks at the door started a dive to the right, going for his holstered gun at the same time. Parker fired, and he ended the dive in a heap and didn't move. Claire froze for just a second at the sound of the shot, but when Parker tugged at her she began to move again.

The other two guards put their hands up over their heads and left them there. Their faces looked cold and white, and Parker could feel the heat of their frustration, but they both had sense enough not to make him kill them.

Parker reached the stairs, and backed down slowly until both guards were just barely still in sight. Then he grabbed Claire by the wrist and went down the rest of the way at a dead run, she teetering and flailing along behind him.

In the lobby there was no one but the night clerk, standing behind his desk with his hands high in the air. But now both guards were at the railing up above, and as Parker angled away from the stairs and headed toward the doors they both opened up. But Claire was too close to him, they were both firing out in front or over his head, trying to rattle him and make him break free of Claire so they could have a good shot at him. He kept her close in, moved fast, went through the doors, and hit the street. To his right Jack French was in the cab of the fake power-and-light company truck grinding the starter.

Parker kept running, straight at the truck. French was too hurried and too harried to see him until he was right there, at the cab. The engine was just kicking over when Parker yanked open the passenger door and shoved Claire ahead of him up into the seat.

French turned his head and went reaching inside his coat, but Parker showed him his own gun and said, "Later. Get us out of here."

French put his hands back on wheel and stick shift, and the truck moved cumbersomely forward. French said, "Where?"

"Left at the corner."

That was no direction at all, except away from downtown, but Parker needed a second or two to think, and French might as well keep them moving along in the meantime.

The trouble was they had nothing set up for a situation like this. They were supposed to have leisure to take the truck to Lebatard's house, more leisure to unload it, more leisure to drive it away someplace else and abandon it and go back to Lebatard's house to arrange the divvy.

This way they were in every kind of trouble. The cops would have been called already, would be getting to the hotel in two or three minutes. Somebody would have to have seen them taking off in this orange truck. They couldn't make any time in it, they couldn't stay on the street with it, they didn't have any place to stash it.

French had made the left. Parker looked ahead, and down the empty bright avenue he saw a neon sign saying PARK. "Head for that," he said. "The parking garage."

"Billy went for his hardware," French said, as though apologizing.

"I figured."

"It was supposed to be quiet."

"I know."

French looked at him past Claire. "I didn't know till today you were back in," he said. "Then it was too late. I promised delivery on this stuff."

French had to be really rattled to do so much talking. Parker said, "Later. When we're clear."

French nodded. "Right," he said, and faced front again.

Claire was still being a zombie, sitting there between them, unblinking, gazing out the windshield.

The parking garage was three stories high. French drove the truck inside and stopped and Parker said, "I'll cool the attendant. Put it out of sight upstairs, leave Claire in it, come down empty-handed."

French said, "We can work something out."

Parker got out of the cab and walked around the back of the truck. The attendant was coming out of his office, looking puzzled, and when he saw the gun in Parker's hand he stopped where he was, snapped to attention like an Army private, looked straight ahead, and said, "Take it all. I only work here, I ain't involved." He was about twenty, thin and sandy-haired, with a huge Adam's apple that kept bobbing as he stood there staring forward.

The truck pulled away up the ramp and Parker said, "Back into the office."

The attendant started walking backwards, still with his arms at his sides and his eyes faced front.

Parker said, "Unbrace, kid. Turn around and walk in there and sit down."

The attendant did what he was told, and Parker stood in front of his desk and said, "My friends and I are going to stay here a while. I'll have an eye on you. If cops come around, nobody's here."

"Yes, sir."

"If cops come around and you spill, you'll get the first bullet."

The attendant looked very earnest and very scared. "I won't spill, sir," he said.

"You can spill," Parker told him, "by looking scared."

"I am scared, sir."

Parker nodded. "That's what you're supposed to be," he said. "But you're not supposed to show it."

"Yes, sir."

"If the cops figure out I'm here, you get the first bullet. Whether you let them know on purpose or not."

The attendant nodded. "Yes, sir. I understand, sir."

"Good."

Parker went back out of the office and shut the door. Through the glass he could see the attendant sitting there, practicing how not to look scared. He needed more practice.

Ahead was the ramp. To the left was a wide fire door leading to concrete stairs. Parker went up these at a run, came cautiously through the door on the second floor, and saw French ahead of him, walking down the ramp. French didn't have anything in his hands and wasn't trying to get down to the first floor unseen.

Parker called, "French!"

French turned, halfway down the ramp, saw Parker, and spread his hands. "I'm clean," he said.

"Why?" Parker asked him. "Why not throw down on me?"

French shook his head. "I can't do it alone," he said. "A quiet heist I could do, but this got noisy. You think on your feet, you'll get out of this. Your fence is dead now, but I've got one. We can help each other."

Did it make sense? Or did French have something cute in mind? Parker said, "Why muscle in on somebody else's proposition?"

"I thought you were out. I thought Lebatard wouldn't be able to get anybody but amateurs, and I figured I could take them. And I told you, I was into my stake. And I figured to take Lempke in with me. I figured he'd come, if the takeover was done anyway, then there'd be two of us to move the stuff."

Parker could see how it might have looked to French, but maybe what he was getting was only something in the vicinity of the truth. He said, "All right. You keep the kid cool downstairs, I'll stay with the truck."

"The broad's flaked out."

"All right. I'll take care of it."

French said, "We scratch each other's backs?"

"Deal," Parker said.

2

CLAIRE WAS standing beside the truck, looking puzzled. When Parker came along she said, "I have to go home now."

"Snap out of it," he said. "We don't have any more time for that."

Calm and reasonable, she said, "We must never speak of that. Will you promise me?"

"I promise," he said. She was still crazy as a loon, but she was being quiet crazy so it was all right. "Sit down in the truck again," he said.

"But I have to go home," she said.

"They want to talk about it there," he told her. "Better stay here."

"Oh," she said. "Then I'll stay for a while."

She climbed back into the cab and sat there, knees primly together, hands folded in her lap. She gazed out through the windshield.

French had put the truck way in a corner of the third floor, out of sight from the top of the ramp. This floor was about half full of cars, all with the keys in them, and Parker went walking around looking for the best vehicle to switch to.

He heard a siren and went to the front part of the building to look. The outer concrete wall was chest-high, and then was open to the air above that. Parker leaned out, looked over the edge, and saw a police car go screaming by, headed toward the hotel. He could hear other sirens now, too, in other parts of town.

It was bad, it was very bad. They'd have the city sewed up in half an hour, and there was no place arranged inside the city to hole up. As to French, Parker thought he could trust him until they were clear, and then he'd have to be taken care of. If they got clear.

He left the wall, walked around some more, and finally found a Volkswagen Microbus down on the second floor. He drove it upstairs, parked it next to the truck, and got out to find Claire collapsed over the truck's steering wheel, crying quietly but desperately.

She looked up when Parker opened the truck door. The madness was out of her eyes, and in its place was pain. She shook her head and whispered, "I didn't know what it was."

"We're in deep now," Parker told her. 'We've got trouble."

"It's all because of me."

"No. French tried a takeover. It's a tough thing to pull off, and he didn't quite make it."

"But Billy's dead, isn't he?"

"Yes."

"That's my fault."

He shrugged. "If you want it," he said, "You want to go turn yourself in?"

She shook her head. "No. I don't want to go to jail."

He was relieved, but didn't show it. If she'd said yes he would have had to kill her, here and now. It would have bothered him; but it would have been necessary, so he would have done it. He said, "You won't be able to go home."

"Why not?"

"They'll identify Billy. Somebody has to know Billy was hanging around you, so the cops'll get to you. Then somebody looks at you and says, 'She's the one was at the hotel'."

"Oh," she said. "You mean, I can't go back at all."

"That's right," he said, watching her.

She thought about it, looking at the dashboard, and then looked back at Parker, saying, "Will you take me with you?"

"For how long?"

She managed a wan smile. "Until one of us gets bored, I suppose."

"Will you break down anymore, like you did tonight?"

"No. That was just a surprise, that's all. The same thing won't surprise me twice."

"Maybe something else'll surprise you."

"I don't think so."

Parker looked at her, and he didn't think so either. He wanted to believe her, because if he believed her he could take her along, but if he couldn't trust her to stay reliable he'd have to shut her now, and he didn't want to have to do that. He said, "All right. We travel together."

"There's one thing," she said.

"What's that?"

"What I told you, about needing seventy thousand dollars. It was a lie."

Parker said, "You mean, you didn't need it for a debt?"

"I didn't need it at all. I didn't *need* it."

"You wanted to build a stake."

"Yes."

Parker grinned. "You work hard," he said.

She smiled uncertainly. "It doesn't change anything?"

"Why should it? I wasn't in this for you, I was in it for me."

"Of course." She smiled more naturally, saying, "I guess I just felt I had to confess something to somebody."

"That's a bad feeling. Don't get it anymore."

"I won't."

"All right," he said. "French is going to be with us for a while. We can use him. Until he feels safe, we can trust him. But you've got to help me watch my back."

"I will."

"Good. Come on, let's switch the goods."

3

HE HEARD sirens again, coming this way. "Keep working," he told her, and went up front again to take a look. They'd been at the job of transferring the cases about five minutes now, and were not quite half done.

Parker looked over the edge. The street was filling up with cops, both in cars and on foot, for several blocks in both directions. Somebody must have seen the truck make a left into this street. Cops were checking alleys, side streets, driveways. As Parker watched, a police car turned slowly and nosed into this building, disappearing from his view.

He trotted back to Claire and said, "Keep it quiet a minute. We've got company. Listen at the head of the ramp. If you hear them coming up, give me the high-sign."

"All right."

He went to the front and looked over the edge again, waiting for them to come back out. If they did come up here he'd have to run for it. Down the stairs if they drove up, or drive down if they came up on foot. There was a blue Porsche parked up there, he'd take that.

If he was taking the car, he'd be able to bring Claire along, but if he had to clear out on foot she'd slow him too much. She'd have to be put out of the way. He didn't think about that, didn't want to think about it, but if the time came he'd do it.

Cops were moving around down there like black models in an electric game. The temptation came to start plinking, to hit every moving shape, to make the street silent and empty again, but he knew the temptation for what it was, an emotional, irrational reaction to being in a tight spot. He kept watching.

It lasted nearly five minutes, and then the dark nose of the police car came turning out into sight again, moving slowly. Parker watched the dark bump of the flasher on the car roof, watched the car turn to the right and drive slowly away.

He waited a minute more, but that was apparently the end of it. The main body of the search had moved farther down the street by now, and the last few cops going by on foot did nothing more than glance into the garage entrance on the way by.

Parker went back over to Claire and said, "All right, it's clear. Let's finish up."

She was better now, almost all the way back to her usual self. She came along with him, and they hurried through the rest of the job of transferring the coin cases.

After a minute, she said, "I had an idea. about French."

"Like what?"

"We drive the truck down," she said, "and we both get out of it and leave the motor running. We make it look as though we don't realize it, but French can get to the truck. So he'll jump into it and drive away, thinking he's got all the loot. Then the police can chase him, and we can get away."

Parker grinned. "That's cute," he said. "But it's no go."

"Why not?"

"In the first place, French won't drive the truck away. He'll stick with us until we're completely out of this town. In the second place, Billy's dead now, so we—"

"Please," she said, and her face had gone chalky again. "Don't say anything about any of that."

He shrugged. "The point is, we need a new fence, somebody to take this stuff off our hands. We could find one without French but it would take time, and we're better off the sooner we get out from under."

"But isn't that dangerous? To keep French around like that. What if he tries to double-cross us?"

"He will. Don't worry about it."

She shook her head. "Whatever you say," she said, and went back to work.

A minute later, as they were finishing up, she said, "I know what you were going to do."

He looked at her. "What do you mean?"

"If the police came upstairs," she said. "I know what you were going to do. But you wouldn't have to. I'd never tell them anything."

He thought about it a few seconds, and then he nodded. "I'll remember that," he said.

4

FRENCH WAS sitting in the office with the attendant. When Parker came in, French looked up and said, "He was very good."

"Fine. Put him out. Sit in for him while I bring it down."

French got to his feet. "Can we move now?"

"We can't wait anymore. It's almost four o'clock. All the cops moved on anyway."

"Good."

Parker started out of the office, then looked back to say, "Don't put him out permanently. Just for now."

"I know. Parker, I'm not a killer. Your boy Lebatard forced my hand back there."

"All right."

Parker went back upstairs. The D.C. license plates that had originally been on the truck were now on the Microbus, with its own local plates stashed away inside. The D.C. plates had been brought along on the truck to be slipped back onto it when it was abandoned.

Claire was already in the passenger seat. Parker got behind the wheel and drove slowly down the ramp. The Microbus moved ponderously because of the weight in back, and Parker had to keep the brakes on hard to prevent it from shooting on down the curving ramp.

French came out of the office as they reached the bottom. He opened the door beside Claire, but Parker told him, "Get in back."

"Right." He shut the door again, opened the side door instead, and climbed in with all the coin cases. "Good idea to make the switch," he said. "That truck was bad news."

Parker drove on out to the street and turned left, back toward the hotel. He took a right turn before getting there, went around Monument Circle, took Indiana northwest, and after half a dozen blocks turned off onto a dark side street and parked at the curb.

French said, "What now?"

"We find a place to hole up." Parker turned to Claire. "You're local. Who do you know that we can move in on?"

Claire frowned. "You mean, somebody to trust? I wouldn't know any—"

"Not to trust. Somebody who won't be missed if they don't show up anywhere for a couple days."

"You don't mean to kill," she said, and a touch of panic showed again behind her eyes.

"No, I don't mean to kill. Killing is something we do only if we don't have any choice."

From in back, French said to Claire, "It was Lebatard forced my play back at the hotel. I didn't—"

"Don't!" She clutched at Parker's forearm, saying, "Parker, please, don't let him talk about it."

Parker said, "Shut up, French. Let her think." To Claire he said, "It would be best if it was a neighborhood where we could park this bus at the curb without it looking out of place."

She was obviously glad at the chance to think about something besides Billy. Nodding, she said, "Someone who won't be missed. That would be someone who doesn't work, who— I know! I know just the one."

"Good. Let's go there."

"She's a divorcée, she—"

"I don't care what she is. Let's get off the street."

5

THE DOOR was finally opened after Parker had been pounding on it for nearly five minutes. "Do you know what time it is?" the bleached blonde in the pink negligee started to say, and then she saw the gun in Parker's hand and she tried, too late, to slam the door again.

Parker pushed in. French behind him. Parker said, "You only get one scream."

She said, "You think I'm crazy?" Her eyes were frightened, her faint double chin was trembling, but she had control of herself.

French said, "It's twenty-five minutes after four. Time for you to go back to bed."

"I didn't know rapists came in pairs," she said.

"Wrong," Parker told her. "We're just going to stay here a while. You be good and we'll be good."

Bewilderment began to take the place of fear. She said, "What is this? What are you two?"

"Men in a hurry," French said. "Turn around and walk back to your bedroom. Slowly."

She said, "Is this somebody's idea of a gag? Did Tommy send you birds around?"

Parker stepped over and took her by the arm, not gently. She had to get a touch of roughness to make her understand this was serious. Holding the arm tight, he pushed her around and shoved her down the hall, saying, "Don't make it tougher on yourself."

"My arm!" She held the arm with her other hand and looked back over her shoulder at him, and he could see by her eyes that she now understood this wasn't anybody's idea of a joke. She walked obediently forward, saying no more, and Parker and French followed her.

Claire had described the apartment layout to them. There were four rooms, all opening to the left off this long white narrow corridor. The living room was first, and then the kitchen, third the bath, and finally the bedroom. A light fixture with a frosted glass globe in the midpoint of the corridor was the only source of illumination at the moment, but when they entered the bedroom Parker felt along the wall beside the door, found a switch, and turned on the overhead light.

The blonde, whose name according to Claire was Mavis Gross, wore a chin patch when in bed; it was lying discarded now on the pillow, where she'd tossed it when she'd gotten up to answer the door. She headed straight for it, tucking it out of sight under the pillow with a quick movement of her hands, and then turned and said, "All right, what now?"

"You lie down. On your face."

"Listen," she said. "You two aren't sadists or anything, are you? I mean, you're not going to cut me up or anything."

"You won't get hurt," Parker told her. "The law's on our tail, we've got to lie low for a while. You do like you're told, everything will be okay." He didn't like taking the time to make this kind of long-winded explanation, but he knew it was better in the long run. She'd be more docile, less trouble, less likely to get panicky, and that meant they could get done with her sooner.

The explanation helped right away. She lay down on the bed, face down as she'd been ordered, and waited while French went through the bureau drawers for something to tie and gag her with. He finally used stockings to tie her wrists and ankles, and went to the bathroom for adhesive tape to close her mouth.

When they were done, they switched off the bedroom light again and went out of the room, shutting the door behind them. French went on into the kitchen and Parker went down the hall to the door and out into the stairwell, where he called down, "Okay."

This had been the arrangement. There was probably no way that Claire could avoid being implicated in the robbery, but she might be able to make some sort of case for herself as a hostage on the basis of where she'd been seen so far. She could claim she'd been waiting in the hotel lobby for a man who stood her up, and that when she left she saw the robbers carrying coin cases, that they grabbed her and held her up in the ballroom, that they had apparently intended to release her after they were finished, and that she'd been taken away as a prisoner afterwards. If this story were to work, Mavis Gross couldn't be allowed to see Claire working in league with Parker and French, so Claire had waited downstairs while the blonde was being put out of the way.

It seemed to Parker that Claire had had a secondary reason for wanting to wait downstairs, that she was still very shaky at the thought of potential violence, but he didn't worry about it. Her control had snapped once, but now she knew it could snap and so she was holding to it tighter than before. She'd be all right.

She came up the stairs slowly, not out of reluctance but out of exhaustion, and when she came close Parker could see her eyes were haggard. "We'll get a couple of hours sleep," he told her.

"How is—how is Mavis?"

"Fine. Tied and gagged, lying in bed. Not hurt, not scared."

"She's probably both," Claire said, "but I know what you meant."

They went into the apartment, and while Parker shut the door Claire went on into the living room, turned a three-way lamp on low, and stretched out on the sofa. "I don't know how I can think about sleeping," she said, her voice already getting fuzzy.

Parker saw she was going under, so he went on into the kitchen, where French had made himself a thick sandwich and opened a can of beer. He looked up from the sandwich and said, his mouth full, "I can never eat before a job. I get a nervous stomach, you know? But afterwards I could eat for a week."

Parker sat down across the kitchen table from him. He said, "We're going to have to work it out."

"I know." French put the sandwich down, swallowed beer, and said, "Let me say my say first."

"I know everything you want to say. You were up tight for cash, you figured you were bucking an amateur operation, everything would have gone smooth except Lebatard tried to draw down on you."

"Then I got rattled," French said. "I should have thrown in with you and Lempke right away, as soon as Lebatard turned it sour. But I wasn't thinking, so when Lempke came through the wall I slugged him. That was stupid."

"The law has Lempke now. And the other two, Carlow and Mainzer."

"I don't know either of them."

"They work around."

French said, "It's too bad about Lempke." But then he shrugged and said, "He won't be the first one died behind the walls."

"The point is," Parker said, "you queered an operation of mine, so I shoudn't let you walk around. But you can set it straight again, bringing your own fence in, so the question is how valuable is that. Enough to keep you breathing, but how much besides."

"Well, there's three of us," French said. "So we split it even."

Parker shook his head. "No, there's six of us. Lempke and Mainzer and Carlow are still in, they've all got contacts that can take their shares. And they'll need it for lawyers and this and that."

"So I get a sixth?"

"You get a sixth." Parker reached out, picked up the beer can, took a swig. "Who's the fence?"

French grinned. "You kidding? He's the only one keeping me alive. I give you the name I'm down the chute."

Parker shrugged. "I can afford to give you a sixth."

"That ought to be enough to stake me. What the hell, I'm in for a sixth. So what do we do now?"

"We wait till eight o'clock, and then you go rent a delivery van."

"Why me?"

Parker looked at him. "Because that's your job," he said.

French said, "I don't like leaving you here with the goods."

"That stuff won't be getting out of this town for a while. Use your head."

French drank some beer, looked at his sandwich, and said, "I wish I'd stayed with it back in the begining. It turned out sweet after all, didn't it?"

"Up to a point," Parker said.

6

UNDER ONE of the railroad bridges over the White River, north of Riley Park, Parker and French worked at transferring the coin cases again, this time from the Microbus to the Dodge delivery van that French had rented. It was nine o'clock on a Sunday morning and nobody was around.

When the cases were all transferred, Parker pulled the D.C. plates off the Microbus and stashed them in the back of the van. Then he and French drove back to Mavis Gross's place, where they'd left Claire still sleeping. Parker stopped in front of the building and French opened his door, but before getting out he said, "I wait one hour. Then I start making trouble."

"I'll be back," Parker told him. "Don't worry about it."

"I do worry," French said. He slid out of the van and shut the door.

Parker drove off, seeing in his rearview mirror French standing there on the sidewalk, looking after him.

Parker drove downtown and went to another parking garage. The attendant here was a moustached Negro asleep in the back seat of a green Lincoln parked beside the office. The Lincoln radio was on, playing a Vivaldi concerto. Parker touched the horn and the attendant immediately woke up and sprang from the car, alert and ready. Parker told him he wanted to leave the van here for a day or two, took the pasteboard the attendant got for him from the office, went back to the street, and walked a couple blocks before he found a booth where he could phone for a cab. He took the cab to within two blocks of the Mavis Gross apartment, walked the rest of the way, and found that French was the one asleep on the sofa and Claire was the one eating a sandwich in the kitchen. She was also drinking coffee, and when Parker came in she went to work making a cup for him.

She said, "What about Mavis? We're going to have to feed her."

"French can do that when he wakes up. Let her get to know his face."

"What about me, Parker?"

"What about you?"

"Do I go back and tell my tragic story? If I'm going to, it better be soon."

Parker said, "What's the other choice?"

"To go with you."

Parker put both hands flat on the Formica tabletop, and looked at his hands as he spoke. "Sometime in the next few days," he said, "I'm going to kill French. You want to be around for it?"

"No. I don't want to hear about it. Never again, Parker. I never want to hear about any of it."

He looked up at her. "What then?"

"I want to be with you," she said. "I know sometimes you'll have to go away and do these things, but those times you can't talk about. Not tell me anything, not before, not after."

"That's how I'd be. Whether you wanted it or not."

"The question is, do you want me?"

He looked at her. "I don't know for how long," he said.

"For a while."

He nodded. "For a while."

She smiled and said, "Then I don't go back, do I?"

"Yes you do."

"I do? Why?"

"We shouldn't both of us be wanted. If you're with me, you can help me, do things I can't do. But not if there's circulars on you, too."

Puzzled, she said, "Then what do I do?"

"You go back. You tell your story, and you hang around two months. Two months from today you go to Utica, New York, Central Hotel. There'll be a reservation waiting for you under the name Claire Carroll. Take the room, and I'll meet you there."

"Parker, is this a complicated way to get rid of me?"

"No. You either take my word for it or you don't."

She said, "You don't have to be complicated, you know. If you don't want me around, you just say so."

"I know that."

"Then—" She stopped, and stared past Parker, and her mouth stayed open.

Parker turned his head, slowly, and saw French in the doorway with a gun in his hand. "You'll never find the truck," he said.

French said, "I'm not out for the whole thing. I can't hang around and play and cat and mouse with you, Parker. When I came in here, before your woman woke up, I called the fence. It's Ray Jensen, in Cincinnati. I told him enough of the situation, and he'll hold my sixth for me. He'll be here tonight and you can dicker with him yourself. I'm clearing out."

Parker watched French's eyes, waiting to see how his chance was going to come, but then Claire said in a tight voice, "Don't do anything, Parker. Please. Don't do anything."

Parker shrugged. "I'll see you around, French," he said.

French said, "We could call it square. You're coming out in good shape."

"If you say so. But let Claire cut out first, she's going back and square herself."

French grinned. "Don't be stupid. She's the only thing keeping you from making a play at me. The two of you just stay here a few minutes. Don't make me nervous. Good-bye, Parker."

"So long, French."

They stayed in the kitchen, Parker sitting at the table and Claire standing near the sink, until they heard the front door slam. Then Claire said, "I'm sorry. But I just wouldn't have been able to take it."

Parker got to his feet. "Wait ten minutes before you leave. I'll see you in Utica."

"Parker—"

He shook his head, and went for the door.

7

PARKER HELD the door barely open, and listened. French wouldn't have had time to get all the way down the stairs yet, but there was no sound, no movement. So he was being cagey and smart.

Where would he be? He wouldn't take a chance on hitting some other apartment; there might be people home, and then he'd have too much to think about all at once. He might go downstairs one flight and wait in the hall there to see what Parker was going to do, but the best bet was that he'd go up instead, wait one floor up, so that if Parker came out after him French would have a clear shot at Parker's back in the hallway. So the thing to do was wait him out.

And there were two further complications. First, there was Claire, whose one taste of violence had made her allergic. Parker could see where that might complicate things a lot in the days to come, but it had its advantages too, in that Claire would be a rare find in a woman, one who would never pry into his affairs. So there was no point aggravating her if it wasn't necessary.

The second complication was the fence. It was set up for him to come here tonight, according to French, and Parker didn't want any ruckus in this building, or even in this immediate neighborhood. So he'd have to wait for French to leave, and then follow him.

He half-expected Claire to come down the corridor after him, asking him not to go after French, but she stayed in the kitchen. That was good; it meant she might have her hang-ups but she wouldn't bug him about them more than absolutely necessary.

French was cautious, more cautious than Parker had

anticipated. When fifteen minutes had gone by with nothing happening, Parker finally left the door, hurried down the corridor to the kitchen, and said under his breath, "Time for you to clear out. Don't look around, don't hesitate, just keep moving."

"All right," she said. She looked composed, but pale. "I'll see you in two months," she said.

"Right."

They went back to the door together, and Parker stood behind it as she went out. He held it so she couldn't close it all the way, and he listened as she went down the stairs and out the door. And then at last he heard the small scuffling sound from upstairs that meant French was going to make his move.

The thing was, French had almost faked Parker out. Parker had been prepared to believe that French was worried enough to pull out, and now he had to remind himself that French was both a pro and hungry. He wanted the whole pie, French did.

Parker pushed the door soundlessly shut, hurried into the living room, and crouched behind an armchair in there, out of sight from the door.

This was another long wait, and he never did hear French come in. French was in the living-room doorway all of a sudden, gun in hand, eyes moving every way at once. He didn't see Parker, and he didn't think Parker was waiting for him, so he moved on down the corridor without making sure.

Parker moved fast and silent across the living room, stepped out into the corridor, and said to French's back, "Right there is good."

French stopped moving. Still facing the other way, he said, "I lied about the fence. I gave you the wrong name."

"Maybe. Drop it."

French's gun bounced on the carpet. Parker stepped forward and put him out with his gunbarrel.

It took one fast guarded phone call to Cincinnati, using French's name, to find out that French had been telling the truth the first time; Ray Jensen was the fence, and was on his way.

It was going to be complicated keeping French alive a while longer, but there was nowhere to stash a corpse here without getting Mavis Gross excited, and Parker wanted her to go on being calm. He was going to have to let her up once or twice between now and when Jensen showed up, and it would be better if she wasn't hysterical.

He went down the hall to the bedroom, opened the door, and found Mavis awake and all in a tangle on the bed. She'd done some thrashing around in a useless attempt to untie herself, and her negligee was now high over heavy thighs.

Parker said, "What's the point of all that? I'm going to untie you now and you shouldn't do anything stupid."

She lay there unmoving while he worked at the tight knots of the stockings around her wrists, and when he had her wrists freed she immediately pulled the tape away from her mouth and said, "What's the matter with you people? You never heard of the calls of nature?"

"That's why I'm letting you up now," he said. "That, and breakfast."

She rolled over and sat up, not bothering about the rumpled negligee. "Thanks a lot."

"Untie your ankles."

"My fingers are all numb."

He had to do it for her himself, and then he said, "My partner's lying out in the hall, but don't worry. He isn't dead. But he wanted to kill you because you saw our faces, and I don't want to get mixed up in any murder rap."

She looked pale, and then she managed a crooked grin and said, "I'm on your side, pal. Will you help me up?"

He took her hand and heaved her up off the bed. She moved clumsily, because of the poor circulation in her arms and legs, and when she got to the hall she said, "You really laid him out, didn't you?"

"I didn't have any choice. Of course, if you lock the bathroom door and start hollering out the window I'll have to think he was right."

"Don't worry about me," she said. "I'm not about to cause anybody any trouble."

"Good."

While she was in the bathroom he used more of her stockings to tie French. He didn't bother with a gag, but when he was done with the stockings dragged French into the bedroom and left him on the floor there.

He went back to the corridor and waited, and after a while Mavis came out of the bathroom. First he saw that she'd put lipstick on, then he saw the way she was looking at him. He said, "Go on in and get some breakfast."

"I was thinking," she said. "You sort of saved my life, didn't you?"

"Maybe," he said.

"I'll have to find some way to express my gratitude," she said. She smiled suggestively. "I wonder if I'll be able to think of anything?"

Parker looked at her, trying to decide whether she really had hot pants or was out to distract him in hopes she could get the drop on him. But the expression on her face wasn't faked, and even if it was he could handle anything along those lines. And it was going to be a long day, waiting for Ray Jensen to show up.

Parker smiled back. "I'll help you think," he said.

8

JENSEN ARRIVED at ten-thirty, and he was surprised to see Parker. "You in on this?" he said. "French didn't tell me."

"French isn't in charge anymore," Parker told him. "Come on in." He and Jensen had met a couple of times before, but didn't really know one another all that well.

Jensen came in warily, saying, "I'm not sure there's anything to discuss, if French isn't around."

"You seen the local papers?"

"I just came in from the airport."

"Come into the living room."

Both Mavis and French were stowed away in the bedroom now, Mavis tied and gagged on the bed and French tied on the floor, and the living room was neat and empty. A faint musky odor still hung in the air around the sofa, where Mavis had expressed her appreciation, and where later on she had expressed her astonishment that Parker should still mistrust her and want to tie her up again.

Parker had gone out early this evening and picked up the local paper, which had put out a Sunday extra in honor of the coin convention heist, and this he now showed to Jensen, who sat down and began to read.

Parker had already read it. He knew that Mainzer and Carlow were in custody, and that Lempke had died of head injuries on his way to the hospital. He knew that the guard he'd shot wasn't dead, but was still on the critical list. He knew the truck had been found in the parking garage and the cops were now looking for the Microbus stolen from the garage. And he knew the value of the coins stolen from the convention had been estimated at three-quarters of a million dollars.

It wasn't from the paper, but from a six-o'clock news broadcast on the radio, that he knew Claire's song and dance had apparently gone over. She was the heroine of the drama, and was said to be helping a police artist sketch the faces of the two missing men. Both the paper and the radio gave it as official opinion that William Lebatard, local coin dealer shot by another member of the gang, had been the brains behind the theft.

Jensen read all there was to read on the job, and then looked up and said, "They always overestimate, you know."

"I'll take two hundred gee."

"That's a lot of money."

Parker shrugged. "We made a big haul."

"You got yourself spread all over the paper," Jensen said. "This may be too hot for me to touch."

"Then I'll call somebody else."

Jensen held up a hand. "I mean," he said, "at the price you quote me. Two hundred thousand dollars is—"

"I'm not haggling. The price is two."

Jensen shook his head. "I can't do it."

"Sorry to waste you time," Parker said, and got to his feet.

Jensen didn't rise. He said, "There's the problem of getting it all out of town. Where is it now?"

"Stowed in a rented truck in a parking garage downtown. It's safe for a couple days. I've got the ticket, that's what I give you for the two."

Jensen frowned. "It would be expensive," he said. "Not impossible, but expensive."

Parker didn't say anything. He waited and Jensen kept frowning. Finally Jensen said, "And there's the problem of cash. I can't put my hands on that kind of money overnight."

"How much time do you need?"

Jensen pursed his lips, fidgeted his fingers, gazed into the middle distance. "Sixty days," he said.

"Where do we meet?"

"There's a place in Akron," Jensen said.

They spent another ten minutes talking, and then Parker turned over the garage ticket and Jensen left. It was agreed that Parker would pick up the money in sixty days at Jensen's drop in

Akron, and it was up to Parker to disburse the money after that. He'd send one quarter to Carlow's contact and one quarter to Mainzer's, not because either of them would turn state's evidence if he didn't but merely because he'd expect them to do the same for him if the situation were reversed.

After Jensen was gone, Parker released Mavis again and they went back to practicing expressions of gratitude. Around two in the morning Parker told her he was going to leave now and she said, "What about your friend?"

"I'll take him along. Will you give me half an hour before you call the law?"

She grinned and patted his cheek. "Do I have to call the law? Did anybody do me any damage? What do I want with a lot of cops?"

"I'll look you up sometime," Parker said, knowing he wouldn't.

"Sure you will," she said.

He went back to the bedroom and untied French's ankles. French whispered, "Parker, you"ll just make yourself trouble. They find my body, that broad will blow the whistle. She won't cover murder."

"Stand up," Parker said, but he had to help French get to his feet because his hands were still tied behind his back.

Mavis was in the bathroom. Parker let French down thc corridor and out of the apartment. They went down the stairs and out to the street and French said, "You've got the whole thing. I heard Jensen's voice, so you've got it all. What's the point of this?"

"You soured a job of mine," Parker said, and walked him down the street.

The streets were quiet and dark in this neighborhood, and empty at this time on a Sunday night. They walked a block and a half and then French spun around, butted Parker in the face with his head, knocked him off his feet, swung a wild kick that glanced off Parker's rib cage, and went running crookedly away down the street, bent forward, trying to run with speed even though his hands were tied behind his back.

Parker rolled to his feet, got his gun out, and fired once. The sound was flat and sharp and solitary in the darkness. French toppled forward and slid to a stop face down.

Parker turned and walked the other way.

9

PARKER, SITTING in a blue Ford across the street, watched Claire go into the hotel, but for a long while he didn't follow her. He'd been staking the hotel for the last three days and as far as he could see no special interest was being taken in it by any cops, but he wanted to be sure. If he could trust Claire he'd find out about it now, and if he couldn't trust her he'd find that out too. As much as possible, he wanted to know which it was before he made his move.

She had arrived just after sunset, and he waited two hours more, until well after full dark. Then he got out of the Ford, entered the hotel through the bar, went from there to the lobby, and stood in a corner of the lobby until he was sure there was no one in it who was going to be trouble. Then he went over to the pay phones, stepped into one, and called the hotel. He watched through the glass as the clerk answered across the way, and when he asked for Claire Carroll there was no unusual reaction. As far as he could see, no signal was given to anybody.

Claire came on almost immediately, and Parker said, "What room?"

"Thirteen oh four," she said.

He hung up, left the booth, and went straight to the elevators. The place was clean, he was sure of that now. He rode up to the thirteenth floor and knocked on her door.